In the pumpkin light amidst waning mirth
Behind a headstone, beneath the earth
Tucked in a grave, there at the bottom
Is where you'll find a shadow of autumn

A SHADOW OF AUTUMN
AN ANTHOLOGY OF FALL AND HALLOWEEN TALES

EDITED BY GWENDOLYN KISTE

A Shadow of Autumn, © 2015

"Salt the Earth" first appeared in *10Flash*, © 2010, and in *Spinetinglers*, © 2013

"The Halloween Girl of Coldsprings" first appeared in *The End of Summer: Thirteen Tales of Halloween*, published by AuthorMike Dark Ink, © 2013

"The September Ceremony" first appeared in Issue 90: Rendezvous of *Danse Macabre*, © 2015

"The Jorogumo's Daughter" first appeared in *Arachnophobia*, published by Thirteen O' Clock Press, © 2015

The stories featured in this book are copyright of their authors. All rights reserved.

No portion of this book may be reproduced, publicly performed, or otherwise distributed without the express written permission of the author(s). Any resemblance of content contained within to persons or events is entirely coincidental.

Cover model: Payden King
Cover photography & interior illustrations: Bill Homan

ISBN-13: 978-1517060749
ISBN-10: 1517060745

Please visit us online at ashadowofautumn.com

FOR ALL THE GHOULS AND GHOSTS AND
GOBLINS THAT CAN ONLY SHOW THEIR
TRUE FACES ON OCTOBER 31st,
THIS ONE'S FOR YOU

TABLE OF CONTENTS

FOREWORD   1

SALT THE EARTH   5
Gerri Leen

THE HALLOWEEN GIRL OF COLDSPRINGS   9
J. Tonzelli

HATTIE'S GHOSTS   19
Scarlett R. Algee

SIMON'S COTTAGE   34
John Kiste

THE HAIRY MAN   49
Julia Benally

THE TRIPLE DARE   69
Miracle Austin

THE BONES OF HILLSIDE   86
Lee A. Forman

ON A NIGHT LIKE DEVIL'S NIGHT   97
Daniel Weaver

THE SEPTEMBER CEREMONY   113
Gwendolyn Kiste

HALL 'O WEEN PARTIE!   123
Troy Blackford

OLD TEMPERANCEVILLE   134
Mike Watt

THE JOROGUMO'S DAUGHTER   142
K.Z. Morano

THE TWISTED END OF VERNON BOGGS   157
Brooke Warra

THE BALFOUR WITCH   163
Tawny Kipphorn

ABOUT THE AUTHORS   167

FOREWORD

Halloween. How lucky are we that such a perfect day exists?

More than just another date on a calendar, this is a celebration that can be, at turns, scary, silly, light-hearted, ghoulish, nostalgic, and unrepentantly modern. For anyone devoted to the unusual, the fall season in general is the most mysterious and beautiful time of year. As the world falls asleep once more and we prepare to face another cruel winter, it's as though nature gives us a final treat to keep us until the next spring. If only it lasted a little longer. Poet Robert Frost might have said it best with the title of one of his most famous poems: *Nothing gold can stay*. Nevertheless, while autumn might be fleeting, that doesn't mean we can't do our best to hold on tight.

So keeping with this all-encompassing love of fall, here in these pages, you'll find stories that span the entire season. Starting in the crisp evenings of September and extending through the glee of trick or treat and the horrors of Devil's Night, these thirteen works of fiction—and one macabre poem—will keep you thrilled and chilled well until November and beyond.

As editor of this anthology, I want to thank the authors for creating such a wonderfully diverse group of stories. From harvest and harvest dances to pumpkin patches and pranks, every facet of fall is on full display for your grisly-loving pleasure.

In the business of publishing, there might be no greater asset than a good proofreader, so I would also like to credit my copyeditors, both of whom are also authors in this book: Scarlett R. Algee and John Kiste. Their invaluable assistance helped to ensure this was the best anthology we could possibly create.

And of course, thank you for being part of this Halloween journey with us. We sincerely hope you enjoy the ghastly wonderment and seasonal terrors in *A Shadow of Autumn*. And may your every day be as joyful and strange as October 31st.

Gwendolyn Kiste
Pittsburgh, Pennsylvania
August 31st, 2015

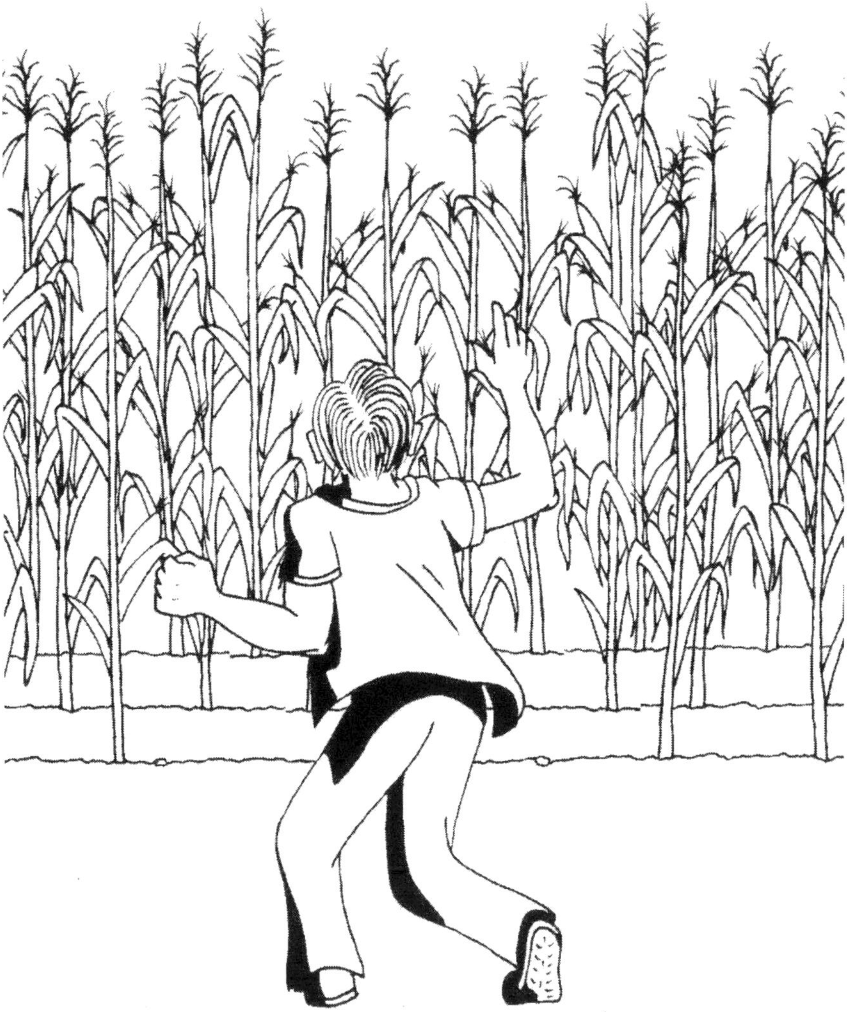

SALT THE EARTH
BY GERRI LEEN

They rise. All night and all day, they rise and I hunt.

It wouldn't be so bad if they didn't keep rising in the middle of my pa's crops. He gets powerful angry every time I salt the earth behind the critters, but I told him I didn't have a choice.

Which is worse, after all: no crops or no family? 'Cause the critters would kill Ma and Sis and even little Jenny Jo, who I think is some kind of cousin. She does favor Pa, though, and Ma tends to treat her pretty unkindly. I've heard some gossipy folks wonder if maybe Jenny Jo isn't Pa's kid instead of his kin.

I can't say I care. Maybe I would have before the critters, but now I'm just plumb exhausted, and those damn things show no sign of stopping. I beat 'em back just enough to give us all a breather. Enough to let us pick some fruit off the orchard trees or fish for the trout that fills the pond.

But the corn? That harvest is getting smaller and smaller each time I go out. Pa cuffed me the last time he caught me ruining his cornfield. Cuffed me hard, too. I couldn't hear for a few days, which made it damned perilous to hunt.

But someone has to hunt. And I'm the only one who sees the critters, so it's up to me.

They're dark and sort of sluglike in appearance, but they can move powerful fast when they want to. I've pointed them out to Jenny Jo and Sis, but they act like there's nothing there. I yelled at Pa to look up from his work to see one slithering down a fencepost next to him, but he just ignored me and the critter. I tried to get Ma to stop her churning long enough to see that she was in mortal danger.

Scared the hell out of her when I shot the thing off the chair next to her. She yelled and told me that if I didn't wise up, I'd be sent to that home where the crazy folk live.

Like I'm the crazy one? I'm not the one churning while a critter is looming.

I'm gonna take me a walkaround now. Find out what the damn things are up to. I can see them oozing over the fences, crawling up from the roots of the corn.

I used to like corn. Used to love the sound it made when it was dry and the ears cut off. But now I hate corn since it shelters my enemy. I'd burn the whole damn field down if Pa hadn't hidden all the matches from me.

Pa is no kind of ally in this fight against evil, but I talk to Doc Pritchett about the critters. He lets me go on and on, and he never tells me I'm crazy or dangerous or scary. He just asks me how the critters make me feel, and then he writes about it in this little notebook he has.

I know that if I die fighting the critters, Doc Pritchett will make sure my name lives on.

I turn to see Pa getting into the tractor, not even paying attention to the critter that's reared up on the seat, waiting for him.

I run. I yell. I even fire the gun I'm not supposed to have in the air.

Pa sits on the critter.

That's how they get in you. That's how they make you evil. You gotta keep 'em off you. Can't let 'em touch you.

"Pa?"

"Boy, what did I tell you about guns?" Pa looks different. Something in his eyes is all off. And the critter is gone. Went up into him when he sat on it.

It pains me to think of how it went up into him. Critters take the nearest hole.

"Pa, just calm down." I love my pa. Even though he yells at me, and hits me sometimes, and pretty much always looks disappointed in me, I love my pa.

But he's not my pa now. He's something else.

He reaches for me and I fire. The body that was my pa's falls, and I see the critter skitter out from under him, hiss at me, and then disappear under the corn.

Damn corn.

I root around in Pa's pocket and find the lighter he uses to get his pipe going every evening. Pa liked to say we were descended from Vikings, and I read somewhere once that Vikings were burned when they died. So I stomp the corn down and roll Pa onto it. Then I light it.

It takes forever to catch. The corn's not young, but still a long ways from the fire hazard that dry corn would be. But it finally does catch, once I think to get some paper to start the flames.

The fire spreads, and it warms me as it blazes because I can hear critters screaming all over the cornfield. I'm killing more of them than I ever have with my normal hunts.

I back away, watch as Pa's body burns and blackens, and I try not to cry at what those things did to him. I'm glad I'm killing so many of them. I'm glad I'm a hunter. I'll keep my family safe.

Ma comes out of the house. Jenny Jo and Sis, too. Ma's screaming and she's got one of Pa's rifles, even though she hates guns.

"It was the critters," I say as I walk toward her. In the distance, I hear sirens. Ma called the fire department.

And maybe the sheriff.

"Ma. I had to do it." I reach out to her, still holding my gun.

"Step away from us, boy." Ma sounds wrong. And I see a critter skittering around in her mouth.

Just before I fire.

THE HALLOWEEN GIRL OF COLDSPRINGS
BY J. TONZELLI

COLDSPRINGS, Ohio — Her nickname was first made popular in October of 1979. Lots of townspeople claim credit for the genesis of the moniker, but it didn't gain notoriety until most people read the headline in that year's local newspaper:

"HALLOWEEN GIRL" VISITS COLDSPRINGS FOR SECOND YEAR; SIGHTINGS ABOUND

From what townspeople are able to piece together, it's mostly accepted that "Halloween Girl" is actually Judy Johnstone, a former and seemingly perpetual nine-year-old citizen of Coldsprings, Ohio, who perished quite tragically in a house fire in 1978—also the year in which sightings of her were first reported. These sightings have occurred on a yearly basis in the week leading up to every Halloween, with this year being the 35th anniversary of her death and subsequent first post-death appearance. What puzzles most people—allowing that mostly anyone would find the idea of a routine and nicknamed ghost-girl sighting, in itself, puzzling—is that Judy Johnstone did not pass away on Halloween, but rather in the middle of May.

More on that later.

It was a mysterious house fire that claimed young Judy's life, the cause of which was never determined. Judy's parents, Gary and Debora Johnstone, were not home at the time the fire broke out, and upon returning, found that their house had burned nearly to the ground. A funeral was held for Judy later that week, her coffin filled with keepsakes and photographs, as her remains were never fully recovered.

Debora Johnstone is now in her late 50s and continues to reside in Coldsprings. She and her husband, Gary, who died of a heart attack in 1999, decided not to have any more children following Judy's passing. Though Judy's death happened more than three decades ago, Mrs. Johnstone still thinks of her daily, and offers up her own theory as to why her daughter chooses the last week of every October to appear.

"She *loved* Halloween. It was her favorite day of the year. I think she misses it. And I think she misses being a kid."

And though she says this with sadness, she often seems grateful to feel her daughter's presence every year. She continues: "She used to love putting on masks and costumes. She used to love pretending to be something unique, or otherworldly. I remember one year I asked her, 'Judy, if you could only be *one* thing for Halloween, what would it be?' and she kinda looked at me funny, and said, 'I would be the sun. I would be so powerful that I could control legions of people. And those people would love me so much that they would give me anything I asked for.'"

Mrs. Johnstone laughs at the memory. "Her dreams were always bigger than life."

"I saw her one year. She was dressed as a witch," says Benny Randolph, a neighbor of Mrs. Johnstone. "She was chasing a black cat down the street. I remember at the time thinking how strange it was that she seemed to be holding one of those large pruning shears, all spread open—you know, the kind for thinning out bushes? But I'm sure it was probably a witch's broom or something. She looked so cute, like she was having a ball. Plus she caught that cat!"

But a witch is not the only costume she's been known to wear. According to witnesses, the Halloween Girl has been spotted wearing several different personas, such as a vampire, a ghoul with rotting skin, and even the Grim Reaper, complete with pale white skin and sunken black eyes.

"She's always had such an imagination," Mrs. Johnstone confirms.

One of the Halloween Girl's costumes, however, does not have her mother's approval: that of the blood-spattered fairy princess. "I haven't seen that one for myself, but I've heard about it," Mrs. Johnstone says. "I don't care for that one. But it's not like I have any say over her costumes anymore. I

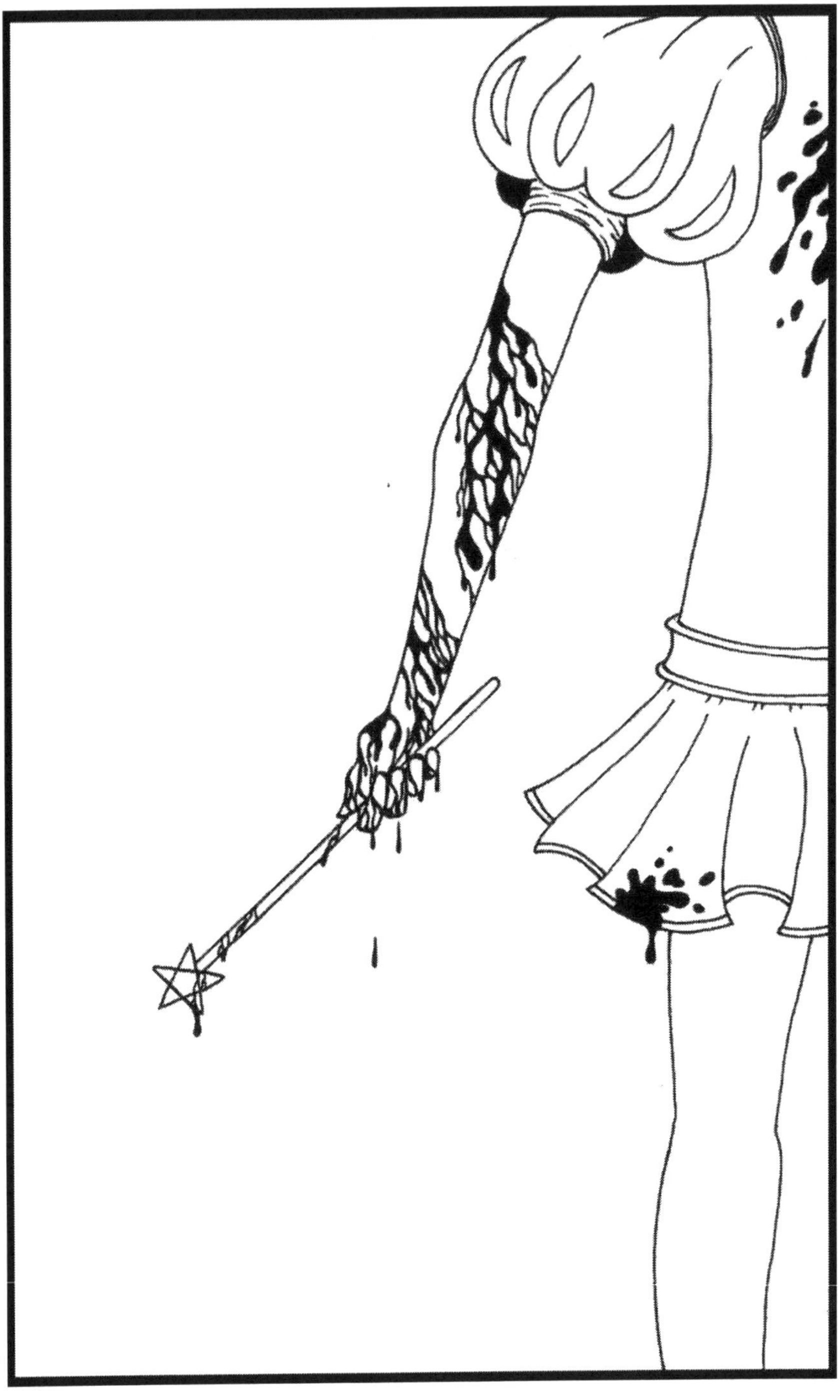

suppose she's earned the right to wear whatever she wants. It's her day, after all."

Despite her periodic gory visage, the Halloween Girl has become an annual staple of Coldsprings, and many of the townspeople look at her as a positive presence to counteract the more disturbing events that seem to spike during the famed October holiday.

"We had us a rogue pack of wild dogs one year, I believe on Halloween night," recalls Mayor Hawkins. "No one ever saw them or heard them, and there were no track marks or paw prints found, but many of the town's pets were discovered mutilated in backyards; blood everywhere, and huge, jagged bite marks covering the poor pets' bodies. But if wild dogs weren't the culprits, then what else could have done something so ferocious and animalistic, you know? That was such an unfortunate time for Coldsprings. But the Halloween Girl... she was our light during times like those, when our morale was low. She just made us see... differently. Things we should have been alarmed by or concerned about—they just didn't seem as important anymore."

In a 1988 interview, another neighbor, Peter Barnes, had agreed: "The Halloween Girl, as weird as it sounds, makes me proud to be from Coldsprings. It makes me feel like our town is unique. It's such a nice place to live that people refuse to leave—even after death!" Barnes was later found murdered in his kitchen on an early October morning, one of his hands jammed into the sink's garbage disposal, his face beaten into an unrecognizable pulp, his body drained nearly of all its blood. The murder was never solved, but Constable McGeehan isn't that concerned.

"It's extremely unlikely that a Coldsprings citizen is responsible for the crime, so the likely scenario is that an assailant committed this murder at random while passing through," says McGeehan. "I'd like to think we'll solve the case one day and give some comfort to the Barnes family, but I know in my heart the Halloween Girl would rather we focus on the bright side. Look, the strong feed off the weak like parasites; unfortunately, that's life. Bad things will always happen to us, but we have to learn to move on and treasure those around us who bring us strength." McGeehan pauses to scratch at two dime-sized wounds on the side of his neck and winces slightly from the pain. He rubs his blood-smeared fingertips together and laughs nervously. "I can shoot holes through bottle caps from 50 yards, but I'm a klutz in the morning with a razor, it seems."

Before another Coldsprings citizen, Father Calloway, passed away under unexplained circumstances, he was one of the Halloween Girl's biggest fans. "She is the brightness in our lives," he said yearly at the pulpit for the special Halloween mass always held in her honor. "I welcome her every year, as I know you all do." In one particular homily, Father Calloway shared with the congregation this story (which also appeared in that week's church bulletin. It has been reprinted verbatim below):

Much like Christians look to the Lord Jesus Christ in times of suffering, we, the Coldsprings community, look to the Halloween Girl in similar times of woe. And much like Christ, the Halloween Girl, too, died untimely, but also gave us reasons to hope, and life for which to be thankful.

It was only one year ago, after having lost a nephew with whom I was very close to anemia, that my faith in the Lord was shaken. I was having terrible and reoccurring nightmares of a monstrous thing feeding from my nephew's body and infecting him with the sickness that caused the disease that claimed his life.

Night after night, when I had this awful dream, I struggled to see the face of the thing that was preying on him. I felt that if I could see the monster and confront it, I could stop the nightmares. And one night... I came close enough to see its terrible eyes and gaping grin for myself. Its teeth were so large that they forced the thing to bear a constant and devious grin, as if it were unable to tuck them inside its horrid mouth.

I awoke in a panic and found the Halloween Girl sitting on my bed. She looked at me curiously, and as I was about to speak, she touched her hand to my cheek, which was flush from the dream. Her hand was cooling, almost ice cold, and I felt an immediate sense of calm. She smiled and bent to kiss my neck. It was quick and perfectly innocent, and just like that, she was gone. I slept soundlessly, and the next morning I awoke to a few drops of dried blood on my pillowcase. I knew at that moment this was the blood of Christ, and the Halloween Girl was not just a phantom or a spirit, but an angel sent from Heaven.

I thank her for that visit, which reinvigorated my soul. I feel as if I have been marked by her, and will now always be protected.

~

Father Calloway died later that week at his home, and five days passed—one of those being the following Sunday, when he was due to preside over the town's weekly mass—before a member of his parish discovered his remains.

"Seeing his body was like a nightmare," says Sister Roberts. "It was torn to shreds, as if a wild animal twice his size had gotten into his room. Blood was... everywhere. But if there's one thing I can safely say, it's that he would want us to look to the Halloween Girl at times like this. She's our shining light. She's so bright... she glows so brilliantly, doesn't she?"

One autumn in the late 1980s was especially hard on the town when a bus full of Coldsprings Elementary School students was found driven off the road—curiously, nearly half a mile into Warren Woods, after having cleared a path through thick trees and somehow negotiating fallen tree trunks, large rocks, and even Jamestown Creek. The bodies of the children had been decimated to the point that some of them could not be identified. The cause of the bus accident and the subsequent deaths of the children were never solved, but the town quickly forgot about the events. Trick-or-treating went on as scheduled the next day, as it was decided the children's funerals would be postponed until after Halloween. Along with the rest of the town citizens who were eager for their annual sighting of the Halloween Girl, the parents of the deceased students could also be found gladly opening their doors to hand out candy to all the trick-or-treaters.

"If you're lucky, she'll come to visit you personally," says one of those parents, Rhonda German, whose seven-year-old daughter, Jessica, had been severed nearly in two from her left hip to her right shoulder. "The Halloween Girl is like contained magic. The things she can show you... they're just beyond description. I miss my Jessica every day, but the Halloween Girl is a good substitute!"

If you ask local Tanya Cardone about the Halloween Girl's latest visit, she will flood you with details about that year's costume, and the glimmering of the girl's large, perfect teeth. "I don't think there's a single person in this town that doesn't look forward to seeing her every year," Ms. Cardone says, and lightly fingers a square bandage covering most of a purple bruise on the side of her neck, just over her jugular vein.

"The town gives Judy all kinds of treats when they see her," says Mr. Randolph. "They leave them outside on their front porch, or sometimes they hand them directly to her if they see her in the street. One year I gave her some ginger pumpkin cookies that I had baked. I guess I left them in the oven for a bit too long, because the edges were a little burned. Boy, she didn't like that! So, instead, I figured I would just feed them to my dog, Jeb, but sadly he went missing that same day."

"Oh, and don't give her peppermints, whatever you do," Mrs. Johnstone adds as she smiles nervously and lightly rubs at the bald stub where her right hand used to be. "She hates those."

"We look forward to seeing the Halloween Girl every year," concludes Constable McGeehan. "In the same way that kids will always go trick-or-treating on Halloween, she, also, will always come to visit Coldsprings that last October week. She knows we'll be here waiting for her. And we'll give her anything she wants. Just like we always have."

~

James Sprenger was a Staff Writer, *Coldsprings Ledger*, Coldsprings, OH, at the time this article was written. James had worked tirelessly for the *Coldsprings Ledger* for 17 years before his recent passing. The publisher and staff offer their condolences to James' friends and family.

HATTIE'S GHOSTS
BY SCARLETT R. ALGEE

A pumpkin. She's a high school freshman, and her social studies project is to carve a freaking pumpkin.

Elaine hunches her shoulders into the southwest wind. She should have been home from school half an hour ago, and her black zip-up hoodie is far too warm for Tennessee in mid-October, but she doesn't care about either. She hadn't asked her dad to take a job in this backwater and uproot her from everything, and the weather matches her mood perfectly: seething. Her teacher, Mrs. Leventhal, had described it as a "lighthearted" project to take the class into the fall break, but to Elaine it's a stupid, *stupid* idea, made even more ridiculous by how desperately she wants to succeed at it.

When she gets to the corner stop sign, she pulls out her phone. Three forty-five. She should be at home trying to pull dinner together—*again*—but she really wants to grab a pumpkin somewhere and get this project started, even if she's got to trudge all the way back across town to Piggly Wiggly.

Elaine stands by the stop sign and looks around, twisting a length of her inky hair around one finger. The street splits here: potholed pavement heading east into the center of town, red gravel heading west into God knows what.

Something flickers in the wind, catching her eye. It's a cardboard sign across the street, fastened to a tree just where the pavement yields to the gravel; it bears a crooked hand-drawn arrow pointing west, and big unsteadily printed letters reading GOSTS 1 HAF MILE.

Gosts. Elaine squints and mouths the word. A bit of gravel crunches under her boots. Is that supposed to be *ghosts*? It must be some hick with one of those dumb haunted barns, she decides, but she really doesn't want to go home right now. She checks her phone again: three fifty-three. Her dad won't be home until after five anyway, and maybe it'll be something interesting. God knows there's nothing else around here.

She clutches her backpack. It's only half a mile.

~

The trek takes her out of town toward a wooded area, past fields of tattered corn stalks and wheat stubble burned into brown smudges. She's a decently fast walker even with her backpack, and after ten minutes, sweaty and mascara-stained, she comes up on a small, weathered farmhouse edged by brown-leaved maple trees that blur into the woods. There's a rickety split-rail fence surrounding it, a rusty mailbox, a bright blue tarp over part of the roof. A lone chicken pecks in the gravel at the edge of the lot.

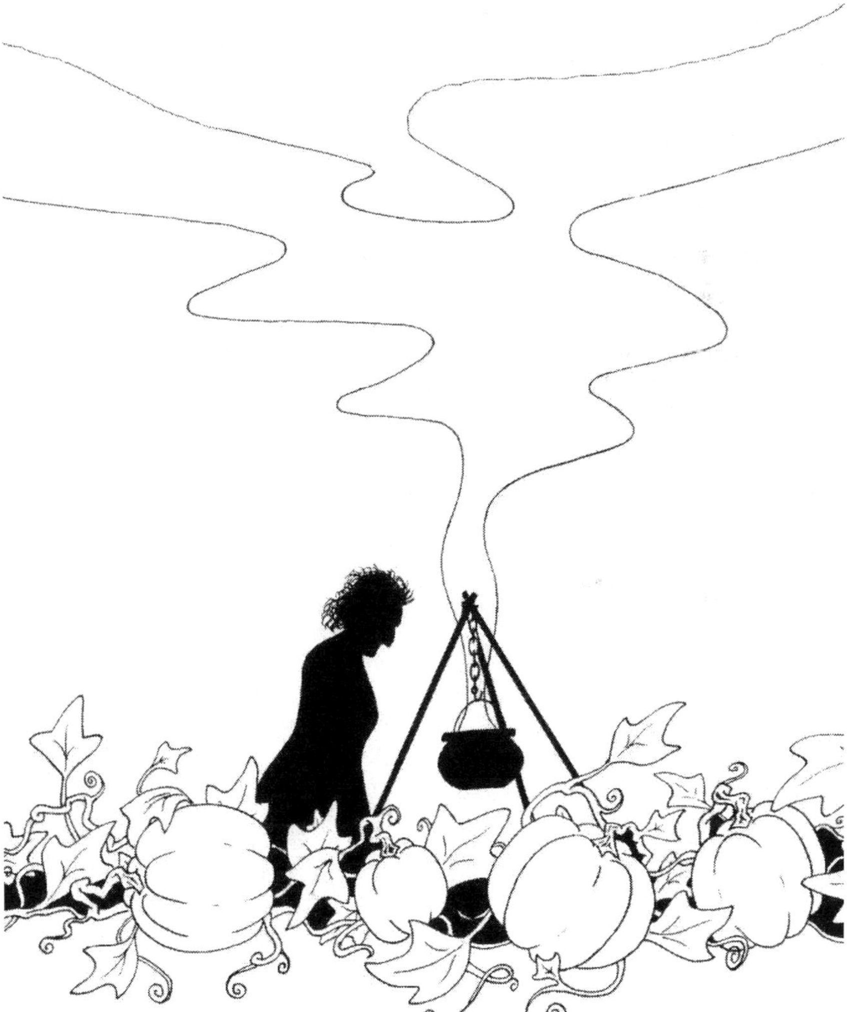

And the yard is full of pumpkins.

Elaine stares, "ghosts" momentarily forgotten. She'd never seen a pumpkin patch growing up in New Jersey. There must be dozens in the carefully planted plots in front of the house—creamy orange and round as basketballs, releasing an earthy sweet scent into the sun-warmed air.

"Wow." In spite of herself, she's impressed. She sets her pack down—carefully this time—and unzips it, fumbling in the inner pocket for the little cash she's got on hand. Four dollars—no, six, she'd skipped the cafeteria slop again today. That's enough, right? Surely it's enough for one that's not too big.

"You need somethin', li'l missy?"

Elaine wads the cash up in her fist. An old woman in a shapeless blue dress and patched half-apron is at her elbow, grinning like a skull, eyes clear green and flinty. Elaine hasn't heard a door open; the woman's been in the yard all along. A German Shepherd trails behind her, bristling but silent, gray-muzzled with age.

"Um." Elaine clears her throat. "Yeah. I need a pumpkin. For school. You know, to carve. Do you sell these?"

"Mmm. You ain't from here." The woman eyes her with the distrust Elaine's grown accustomed to seeing, but nods gruffly. "Carvers, up this way."

She walks toward the house. Elaine follows a little uneasily, looking around more. The pumpkins that grow in the plots near the house are a little larger than the ones she'd first spotted, their orange hue starker, and there's no hint of sweetness here. Instead, the odor in the air is meaty and faintly rancid, like cooked beef gone just a bit off. She wrinkles her nose, then catches a whiff of smoke and tracks it to a fire pit not far from the porch, overhung by an enormous black iron pot that's the source of the smell.

She's a witch, Elaine thinks and chokes back a sudden giggle. No, that's kid stuff. Just some old lady cooking outside because she's too poor to have air conditioning. She shifts her attention back to the pumpkins. "How much are they?"

"Fifty cents a pound. Dollar for them pie-makers you was eyeballin' back yonder." The woman coughs and spits into the dirt. "I'll go get the scales while you're pickin'."

"Wait," Elaine says, remembering herself. "Do you know anything about some ghosts? I saw a sign—"

"Hah!" The woman laughs, and it's an unpleasant sound. "Seen my sign, did you? My special ones, them are. My Ghosts." The capital letter is practically audible. "I hope you brung more money, li'l missy, them's five dollar a pound."

"Five dollars?" Elaine blinks. "Pumpkins? Ghosts are pumpkins? Why the hell would they cost so much?"

She catches herself too late and shuts her mouth so fast her teeth click, but the old woman just responds to the profanity with another cough and another ghastly grin. "Growed special. Come on around behind the house, I reckon you can look."

Elaine hesitates. She only has six dollars, and a one-pound pumpkin won't be big enough to carve properly. Still, she can satisfy her curiosity. Her tiny sheaf of cash gets shoved into a pocket of her jeans. "Okay."

She lets herself be led, lifting her feet when she's told—"Mind them roots, ol' oak stump under the grass here"—and finding that the old woman's more nimble than she looks. The back of the property is far messier than the front. Rounding the house, Elaine sees a yard that's mostly bare dirt and mud, crossed by the fallen trunk of a lightning-scarred maple. She only sees the pumpkins when she's walked past the tiny slumped back porch into a solitary grassy patch.

"White!" Elaine gapes. "They're solid white!"

The old woman cackles and rakes her gray hair up wild. "Surely! Ain't that somethin'!"

Elaine squats at the edge of the grass. There aren't many pumpkins here, but they're just as full and hefty as their orange brethren, and pale as fresh snow. She touches the nearest one: warm, despite lying in the shadow of the house. The rind has a peculiarly leathery texture, and she could swear the supple vines have a pink tinge. "How do you grow them like this?"

"Aw, pumpkins come whitish natural," is the drawled reply. "Started these from seed, got 'em to grow seedless now. It's all in what you feed 'em, that's their supper I got stewin' in the front yard."

Elaine's not listening; she's too busy seeing a perfect blank canvas in her mind. She's got to have one of these, cost be damned. There's no way any of her hayseed classmates are bright enough to think of this.

She jumps up and dusts herself off. "You're right. I don't have enough money yet. But I'll be back, so don't you sell any of these till I get one. I want to be first."

The old woman just smiles.

~

She gets home to find her dad's beaten her there.

Elaine groans at the sight of his car in the driveway and dredges up her phone: four fifty. He's never home from the agricultural extension office before five fifteen. Taking a deep breath, she mounts the steps and drops her backpack inside the open doorway of the screened-in porch. As soon as she walks into the house, she can smell vegetable soup.

"Dad? Dad, what gives?"

"I'm in here," he calls from the kitchen. He's standing over the stove making grilled cheese sandwiches—the kind, she notices a little guiltily, with too much butter and no crust. The perfect ones, with a pot of veggie soup bubbling on the next burner. "Lainey," he says, sighing, "where have you been?"

She bristles a little at the nickname. "I went walking. It's been a rough day."

He flips a sandwich. "Fifteen-year-old girls shouldn't have rough days."

Elaine sinks into a chair at the kitchen table and pillows her head on her arms. Fifteen-year-old girls shouldn't have mothers who've been dead five months, or fathers who wither and hide. She studies her father's profile, the lines around his mouth and the gray in his hair that weren't there before her mom's car crash.

I miss Mom too, she wants to say, though she bites her tongue. It's a taboo subject.

Instead, she fiddles with the skull-shaped zipper tab on her hoodie. "Um. Look. I have a school project and I need a little money."

Her father's not frowning yet, but she can see it starting in his eyes long before it reaches his face. "What kind of project?"

"For social studies. I have to carve a pumpkin." Elaine looks up hopefully. "I only have a week."

"For social studies," her father repeats dully. "Why—no, never mind. Fine. We'll go to Kroger this week and get one."

"Dad, no." She pushes back from the table. "I found a place outside town that sells white ones. I want a white one."

He's pulling soup bowls from the cabinet. "You went out to Hattie McClain's place? I can't even get you out of your room in the morning!"

"*Dad,*" Elaine grumbles. "It's not far and it's important! This is for school and it's my chance to prove I'm more than just the dumb new girl!"

"Lainey—"

"It's been two months, Dad! Two months and to these hicks I'm still just the 'weird' one." She makes finger quotes around the word. "My mom's dead, my dad's a Yankee, I'm a 'vampire' with a funny accent—"

"Elaine." He plunks a bowl down in front of her. Soup droplets bounce out onto the tabletop. "I'm not talking about this right now." His voice has gone cold and flat. "We'll see about your project. We'll see. Later. Not right now."

He drops a spoon beside her bowl. "Now eat and go clean up and do your homework."

~

Elaine has geometry to do, but she's pushed that aside. She can't concentrate on it now.

We'll see. Of all the answers her dad could have given her, it had to be the one that means 'no' without making him actually say it. It's practically the only way he's responded to her requests since June. Allowance? We'll see, no matter how many chores she's done or meals she's cooked. School supplies? We'll see. Jesus, she only got clothes for the start of the new school year because her Aunt Tina had taken her shopping before they'd left Jersey for this podunk.

She sits down at her cheap plywood Wal-Mart desk and thumbs her phone. One email to Aunt Tina, and within an hour, she'd probably have more money than she needs sitting in her PayPal account, but there'd also be a phone call to her dad about why he's not providing properly, and Elaine doesn't want to deal with that right now either. Besides, she's pretty sure this Hattie McClain doesn't take PayPal.

She drums her fingers on the desktop over the notes she's made for her pumpkin. Cut out the top and scoop out the goo. Cut out angled eyes, lowered brows, mouthful of jagged teeth. Cut drawings into the topmost layer of the rind—crooked houses, leafless twitchy trees, arch-backed cats. Rub powdered charcoal into the lines and wipe the excess off. It'll look awesome. She's Googled it all. The only thing she needs now is the pumpkin, which takes money, and with the mood her dad's been in, she'll probably have to steal the damned thing.

Elaine's drumming stops. She's never done that before. Sneaking out, of course, just to be alone with her thoughts; her dad never comes into her room even to say good night, and this rinky-dink town is so quiet, she knows she's perfectly safe. But not stealing. A pumpkin. A fucking pumpkin.

The thought makes her giggle, but not for long. There's no way she'll pry fifteen or twenty bucks out of her dad, not when he'll argue she can buy one for three at Kroger and paint it. And those white pumpkins have such soft, flabby stems—her fingers twitch, recalling the oddness of it—that she's positive her craft scissors will do the job. Her scissors, a small flashlight, the compass on her phone. That should be enough.

She'll need her hoodie and her boots, and probably her black sweatpants, to keep from being seen. This is a single-story house, so there's no climbing down from the window, and since her dad always goes to work and leaves her alone to walk to school, she can sneak out and grab a pumpkin, sneak it back in and carve it, and get it to Mrs. Leventhal with no trouble at all.

No one will even notice she's gone.

~

Thank God for iPhone compasses and Google Maps to keep her from having to retrace her steps. Elaine's pretty sure she'd be lost by now otherwise.

It's so *dark* out here. Haven't these people heard of street lights? Apparently not, since no one's told them gravel roads aren't the in thing anymore. Elaine shivers despite her too-warm clothes. Having so many stars overhead when she looks up is dizzying, but using the flashlight to keep from stumbling over a lump of fresh roadkill makes her feel too visible. Except for brief snatches to check her phone, she's made the trek by sheer memory. Her calves ache.

Elaine leans on Hattie McClain's fence for a moment to catch her breath, then begins to pick her way through the front yard. The woman's got a front porch light on, yellow and very dim, and all the windows are dark. Even so, Elaine shies away from the house as much as she can until she reaches the back. The tiny patch of white pumpkins is visible even with mere starlight to illuminate them.

The one she'd picked out earlier is still here; Elaine recognizes the shape. She squats in the grass as she had before and almost immediately is hit by nausea. The weird meaty smell from before is suddenly all around her, only now it's shit and blood and spoilage, magnified by the day's heat seeping from the ground. Flies are buzzing, and something squelches under her feet. She pinches her nose shut with one hand and turns on her flashlight with the other. The pumpkins are swimming in a stew of rotten meat, moldy scraps, and thick pink liquid. The patch looks like a crime scene.

Elaine gags and spits, breathing through her mouth as she lets go of her nose and fumbles out the scissors. She'll have to work fast.

She gasps in air and grabs the pumpkin stem, but it feels different now—thicker, almost veiny. She squeezes gently and gets the impression it's full of liquid. Wincing, holding her flashlight in two fingers, she finds a thin spot in the stem and slips the scissors around it. Another squeeze, and the stem tears with a ripping sound, and fluid *gushes* over her hands.

Elaine yelps and jumps to her feet, dropping the scissors. Her boots are covered in liquid stench. She vomits helplessly and stumbles back.

Something explodes beside her.

It's the back door, slammed open against the house. Before she can gather strength to run, Elaine is pinned in place by a powerful flashlight beam and the muzzle of a double-barreled shotgun shoved into her belly. Hattie McClain leans over her, looking enormous in her wrath.

"Well. Li'l missy. Out-o'-towner," the old woman growls, jabbing her with the gun. "I reckon you thought you'd make off with one o' my babies."

"Please." Elaine's voice squeaks. "Please don't shoot me."

"Why not? You think you can hurt one o' my babies

without me knowin' it, when I feed 'em from my own hands? You think they ain't gonna cry for me?"

"You're crazy." Elaine sobs, which gets her a harder jab. "*Please!* Just—please let me go! Let me go home and I swear I'll never bother you again! I'm sorry!"

"Sorry, all right." Hattie grunts. "Get your ass in the house 'fore I blow it off."

Elaine stares. "What?"

The shotgun gets lowered, but only for Hattie to tuck it under her other arm and seize Elaine's collar. "In the house," she repeats. "You're gonna feed my babies."

~

Brad Stanton drives down the red gravel road with his heart somewhere in his gut. Two weeks since he'd gotten the call at work that Elaine hadn't shown up at school. Ten days since her craft scissors, her phone, and a flashlight had been found deep in the woods, wrapped in the filthy, bloodied remains of her hoodie. Since then, the police haven't given him anything to go on but the opinion that his daughter had been unhappy enough to run away, and that the findings are just things she'd left behind to throw them off the trail. They've had an Amber Alert issued.

That doesn't account for the blood. He suspects they simply don't care. He's an outsider, after all.

He finds a spot along the side of the road to park and barely squeezes in. Tomorrow's Halloween and Hattie McClain's pumpkin patch is swamped with people making their last minute purchases. A sign on the fence is scrawled with CUT YOR OWN; the little farm is so picked over already, he's afraid he won't find what he wants.

There's one white pumpkin at the back of the house, shining like an incandescent bulb in its trampled patch of grass. Brad looks it over unhappily. It's a little withered, with a jagged black mark in the stem as though someone had tried to cut it loose and the wound had healed. He'd only brought a penknife, but he takes it out to saw at the blemished stem. Elaine deserves better, she deserves *perfect*, but this is all he can do.

Back home, poorer by eighteen dollars and richer by one strange pumpkin, Brad sets the thing on the kitchen counter atop a protective bed of newspaper and gets a bowl to dump the innards in. He had to buy a carving knife since he's never done this before.

He makes a cut. A circle of the rind lifts out easily with a tug on the severed stem, and he reaches in to start scooping, realizing only belatedly that he should have worn gloves or used a spoon. There's little pulp inside, much less than he'd expected, but the texture of it is unusually fleshy and slippery, more like thick decaying meat than the contents of a gourd. Brad grimaces and dumps the first handful into the bowl, wincing at the odor of sweet rot and trying to ignore the warmth of the stuff. He just scoops and pulls and discards, holding his breath, unable to keep from wondering if he should take this bowl to work tomorrow. The workers at the extension office have been puzzling over these white pumpkins for years.

There's one last big handful of pulp inside the shell. Closing his eyes, Brad gathers it in his hand and pulls it free. Its fibers stick to his fingers and he shakes it off toward the bowl without looking, only paying attention when he hears the *plink* of metal on metal. A few strands of dark string are atop the bowl of pulp. He winds a finger in them gingerly and lifts an object out and begins to scream.

He's holding a skull-shaped zipper tab, tangled in a length of black hair.

SIMON'S COTTAGE
BY JOHN KISTE

The first sounds of laughter arced through old Simon's kitchen window very like the slanting rays of the late afternoon sun. The smell of dead leaves, rotting pumpkins, and hot apple cider filled the air. The celebration of waning October was again upon him. By nightfall the trick-or-treaters would attack en masse. But, as always, he would be steeled against them. His annual ritual was no less exacting than the carefully planned routes of those neighborhood children who took this night every bit as seriously as the ancient druids—albeit for different reasons.

The Celtic leaders of olden times offered up blood sacrifices in hopes of coaxing back the pleasant gods of summer warmth. The scheming pagans of the suburbs charted their nightly path while dreaming of full candy bags and bloated bellies. And the old man... his plots to keep the scoundrelly beggars at bay were no less intricate.

He rose from the unvarnished table on his tiny, spindly legs and moved to the dusty, uncurtained window. Far down the quiet street he could see the first of the masked entourage marching from door to door. Even under their heavy red and green devil and witch make-up, he recognized them as little Bobby and Emily Fitzpatrick. They had lived on the block all their lives; no fear of those two venturing to the end of the lane, where his drab cottage huddled next to the cemetery gates like a long-dead watchdog. Little Bobby and Emily would give the graveyard and the cottage a wide berth.

But there was always danger from the novice intruders; youngsters who had but recently moved into the neighborhood, or who had never before been old enough to go candy-hunting quite this far afield. And occasionally a giddy goblin would forget himself in the heady gaiety of the night. Forget himself, and find himself knocking at old Simon's door before he comprehended what he was doing. This would happen occasionally—but not often. And never twice.

No, never twice. Simon would see to that. It wasn't that Simon just didn't answer the door, albeit he never did. It was that the tiny, cadaverous old man *would* be waiting, and one never knew where. He could contort himself into a ball beneath the porch, or take advantage of his very small stature by secreting himself in the niche between his front archway and his shuttered bay windows.

Wherever he might hide, one would never see him until he sprang forth, swearing and growling and frothing in his fluffy gray beard like a rabid wolf. He would howl and scream and spit and stretch forth his bony hands as though intending to tear the life from the luckless interloper. That one would never linger, assuredly. That one would turn and pump his or her sheet-clothed legs down the walkway with the speed of a stubby puma, and would keep running until his or her little heart threatened to pound free of his or her heaving chest.

No adult had ever seen old Simon chase a candy-ghoul beyond his own property line, but the now-rife legends argued the extent of the madman's perimeter. Indeed, Bobby Fitzpatrick yearly raised the hairs of his companions' necks by relating the tale of the time old Simon had loped in pursuit clear to the boy's own porch before disappearing in a livid flash. Not to be outdone, Tom Geedy, the wrinkly welfare wiseass from three blocks over, would always counter with his version of a chase by Simon that only ended the following dawn when the morning rays forced the evil old man to transform into a scrawny bat and flutter off to the west.

Simon had heard all the yarns. As long as the child-devils avoided his house like the Black Death, it mattered not to him the truth or fiction of the tales. He passed through the dreary living room to the front door and out onto the crumbling porch. The autumn wind was kicking up a bit, and wisps of frost-clouds were moving in from the north, feebly threatening to obscure the last rays of pale sunlight, but the early evening was not yet cold. Simon stomped down his steps and reached beneath the porch for his sign and his mallet.

Several children dancing down the street stopped dead in their tracks to watch him pound it into the dirt. "No Trespassing—Private Property". Old Simon looked up at them; one of them raised his mask to the position of visor and stuck out a tongue stained green with peppermint. Then all the goblins fled in a swarm of giggles.

Simon grunted, stumped back through his one-story cottage, and taped up his customary back door sign: "Violators Will Be Eaten". Then he was forced to sit and rest a moment. The old man liked to think he was still in top form for his annual routine, but in truth he was getting a little rickety about the edges. Some year soon the legions of licorice-loving heathens would wear him out—but not this year. No, not this year.

He resumed his post at the window; observed with a scowl as the little Fitzpatricks linked up with their cohorts near the turn far up the street. His gaze slowly shifted to the fluttering yew hedges that lined the cemetery. Some prankster had smashed two jack-o'-lanterns at the wrought iron gates. Their yellow brains mingled together; their oozing, crumpled smiles and squinty eyes watched him from the cobbles.

Dim remembrances of far-off trick-or-treats brushed past his mind, tapping at the wispy chords of recall. Each year the sights and sounds of Halloween would softly rap upon his faded memories. The tart of burning leaf piles would mingle with the musk of just-turned earth and the brashness of roasting ears of fresh corn. The chill wind would hint of icy blasts to come; and the brown, crimson, and golden foliage would foreshadow the bleak, bare branches of December.

All these needles to his consciousness would push Simon far backwards in his own mind's eye. He would, for an instant, see and hear and smell these things as a child, when such staples of the season affected those senses so very differently. As a child, the rapid falling away of life from all the earth had terrified Simon. It was as though all of nature had chosen to peel back its thin façade and reveal a black, dead soul. The fear had clutched at Simon, and vestiges of its effects on him clung to his heart even now.

But in all his musings of present, he never felt fear. He stroked his fluffy gray beard as he considered this; ran his fingers through the whiskers as he always did when pondering such thoughts. The fear itself lived no more—only the shadowy remembrances of it—and even those remembrances were tainted by his strongest recollections of October youth. The tastes of the night: cloying but succulent chocolate caramels, shimmering candied apples, rich sweet draughts of cider, hot and spicy pumpkin pie tossed up with thick dollops of homemade whipped cream. And above all, the infinite varieties of candy. Oh, the wondrous variegated assortments of sweets!

How could one fear when such memories held dominion over all others? When memories were all he carried about with him, how could he feel the stark terror of devils and demons that was the hallmark of this night? It seemed unfair that the sense of crawling, pulsating horror could no longer pervade him. What was the Celtic festival without it? No matter, that was many years ago; he was growing old and weary, and it was night...

~

The skeleton rose from behind the cold marble gravestone like an inflatable ghost in a carnival chamber of horrors. Those creeping among the markers jumped back in sudden fright, and Emily screamed. Her brother instantly clamped his hand over her mouth. Tom Geedy swore.

"Jeez, you scared the piss out of us!" spat the last fellow, the one dressed as a Caribbean pirate. "Anyone farther on?"

The skeleton stepped silently into the group and shook his head. The moon danced occasionally about the tombstone, but the clouds from the north had arrived to darken the scene. A final straggler, plump in vampire cape and fangs, whispered from beyond the yews. "Wait up, guys."

"Shh!" retorted the other five.

The amateur Dracula struggled through the hedges and ran, crouching to where the group lay in sight of old Simon's cottage. "Hi, annual cohorts," he giggled as red Karo syrup dribbled from the corners of his mouth.

"Shut up!" retorted the other five.

Not taking offense, he tried another tack. "There's our target, men. Should we synchronize watches?"

"Shhh!"

Now Dracula showed disappointment. "Ah, you guys

are just jealous 'cause you know my brains dictate I should lead this group."

Tom Geedy reached out his homemade octopus arms and embraced Dracula angrily. Then he whispered violently in the cringing vampire's ear. "Listen! In the first place, the only brains you gonna have in a second will be smeared on this rock if you don't quiet down. In the second place, we don't know each other from Adam." It was true; Geedy knew Emily and Bobby, but although the same six of them showed up every year, the rest were strangers to each other. Indeed, the only thing they had in common was a desire to do as much damage as they could to old Simon's cottage—without getting caught. "In the third place, the skeleton leads."

Dracula fidgeted, nearly to tears, but he would not back down. "Why?"

Tom Geedy paused. "Why? Because... because he always has."

"Yeah," hissed Emily, turning a green nose toward them.

The pudgy face was unconvinced. "So? I have a claim. That shriveled old creep Simon once—uh—uh—once clawed the seat out of my best costume. Yeah. That skeleton can't top that story. Hell, he always comes as that skeleton..."

Tom's grip tightened, mainly because he himself had been a homemade octopus for three years running. "Hey, old Simon once chased me to the junkyard on the outskirts of town..."

"We know," groaned the pirate, pushing his eye patch

from one eye to the other. "At dawn he flew away. Maybe he also turned you into a real octopus under that mask."

"Yeah," countered Emily, earnestness in her voice as she pointed to the leader. "And maybe *he* is a real skeleton under that mask. We don't know. Come on, Skelly. What is your claim to leadership?"

The little skeleton whispered, in his always soft but somber voice, "He imbued my very soul with the terror of evil."

Without thinking, the cherubic vampire said, "What's imbooed?"

"Ha!" laughed Tom Geedy. "Your brains dictate shit. The skeleton wins."

That seemed to settle the matter, and the costumed guerilla force began their final advance. As they crawled under the last yews, Tom nudged Bobby. "What is imbooed, anyhow?" Bobby shrugged, and the pirate and the skeleton laughed. Dracula puffed and quietly whined as he brought up the rear.

Now the little team faced the open expanse of yard between the cemetery and Simon's outer shrubs. A false move could be fatal. "Leave the candy bags here," whispered Tom. "Everyone put your weapons into Skelly's bag." Skeleton unfolded the arsenal bag which he always kept stashed under his cloth ribcage, and they all dumped their arms into it. From the candy bags they extracted Indian corn, chalk, soap, paraffin, screwdrivers, and several rolls of toilet paper. All was funneled into the single bag.

"Ready?" whispered the skeleton, always very quiet. "Let's teach the old ghoul to imbue us with anything!"

A silent cheer went through the ranks, and they dashed, two by two, into Simon's rotting shrubbery. The wind kicked up and, far off, a dog barked. The scheming half dozen lay breathless on the frosty ground. Only one dim reading lamp glowed within the bowels of Simon's dismal fortress. The moment had arrived.

The skeleton took charge. "OK, you—" pointing to Bobby and Emily, "the witch and the devil. Just wearing make-up, so you can see better. You do the T.P.ing." And Skelly passed them the White Cloud. "The pirate and the vampire—here." They got the screwdriver. "Eight arms comes with me. We'll corn the porch. Meet back here in three minutes for window waxing. Go!"

The little Fitzpatricks sidled off to the sparse elms and began stealthily hurling the soft rolls over the branches. Cottony white and patterned print streamers smoothly leapt through the limbs, periodically snatching a glint of far-off streetlight. The team moved furtively from tree to tree and bush to bush, adding a decorative touch of outhouse to each plant they encountered. The last of the rolls they wrapped about the No Trespassing sign.

Mewing like a near-mute lost soul, Dracula began to protest his lot, but the Caribbean swashbuckler pushed the caped cherub to his knees and stepped onto his back. From this position "Captain Blood" could easily reach the rain gutter on the low-slung cottage. As he gingerly began loosening it with the slotted screwdriver, the vampire whined, "Why am I always on the ground? My mom says if I get mud on my knees this year..."

The pirate squatted down on his perch, and the tip of the fake saber secured to his waist touched Dracula's neck. "Feel that. That's the screwdriver," he whispered, lying. "One more word, bat brain, and your throat gets a new puncture." Dracula shut up, pulled half a candy bar from his sleeve, and began munching. In another minute, the pirate carefully pulled the gutter loose from the downspout and let it dangle halfway to the ground.

The skeleton and the octopus, both wearing clumsy masks, had gotten the relatively simple task of spreading feed corn kernels across the porch. Most Halloweeners would hurl handfuls and run, unmindful of the clatter. Not this group. They spread the hard maize bits quietly and thoroughly into every corner, for years of practice had pointed out each squeaky board on the old porch. They could venture no noise just yet, for the riskiest task was yet before them.

In three minutes, the ghoulish coven reconvened. "Good," murmured the skeleton. "Everyone dig in for wax and soap."

As the group reached into the arsenal bag, the vampire grunted, "I dunno why I keep coming back..." Three of Tom Geedy's fake tentacles pummeled him to silence. The little devil's legion followed the skeleton from window to window, and their mark was clearly visible on each pane as they left it behind. Just beside the living room glass, the skeleton halted the group as the distant church clock sounded ten.

"Go on," waved Tom Geedy, and one of his tentacles dropped to the ground. "What ya waitin' on? There's curtains at this one."

Skeleton drew in his breath. "OK, ready...?"

The rest drew in their breath, too, but not in anticipation. The living room light switched on. Old Simon's silhouette could be clearly seen pressed against the curtains.

"Oh, shit!" said two of them, as the group flattened itself against the house. They stood silent, hearts racing, pulses pounding, and bodies shivering—not with the cold.

The figure behind the curtain did not move, but it was quite close to the window. If they ran they would be seen. Could they make it to the cemetery yews? Yes, if the old man came out the *door* after them. But they had often debated of Halloween nights whether this was, after all, a man. Would he perhaps crash right through the glass upon them? Or, more horrible yet, reach though the walls as though those walls were mere mist and pull their shrieking bodies into the midst of the crumbling shingles and plaster? What was this creature capable of?

The pirate started to move. Skeleton clutched his arm. "No, don't break and run," he warned in an undertone. "Legends say he's faster than any demon."

"He *is* a demon!" countered the pirate in a hushed snarl. He nearly left the wall again, but the others emphatically shook their heads, and he finally settled back into the shadow of the eave.

For the longest two minutes in earth's history, as their teeth chattered and their knees rattled, the figure stood behind the curtains, outlined evilly by the backlight. Then suddenly, just as Emily Fitzpatrick knew she was going to scream, the light clicked off. There was a collective exhalation. Another of Tom Geedy's tentacles dropped off. "That was close," someone sighed.

"Let's go."

The gaggle of fiends crouched and ran, not looking back until they reached the line of yews. There they dropped and whipped around onto their bellies beneath the hedges so they could see the newly "decorated" cottage. Again they drew their breath in amazement. The pudgy little vampire still stood at the window—not frozen with fear but calmly polishing off his candy bar. That done, he pulled out his wax stick and scrawled "Sucker!" on the dark, curtained glass. Then he nonchalantly tossed down the wax and strolled to where the rest lay—stunned—in the shrubs.

"Next year," he said mildly, "I lead." And he left them. Their mouths wide, for a long time the others watched him march up the dark street. Then they laughed. There was all the relief of stark terror in that laughter. They laughed so hard two more of Tom Geedy's tentacle arms snapped off.

"What you comin' as next year, Geedy?" giggled Emily as she bopped the hideous homemade cuttlefish mask. "A slug?" At that the pirate laughed so hard he had to wipe

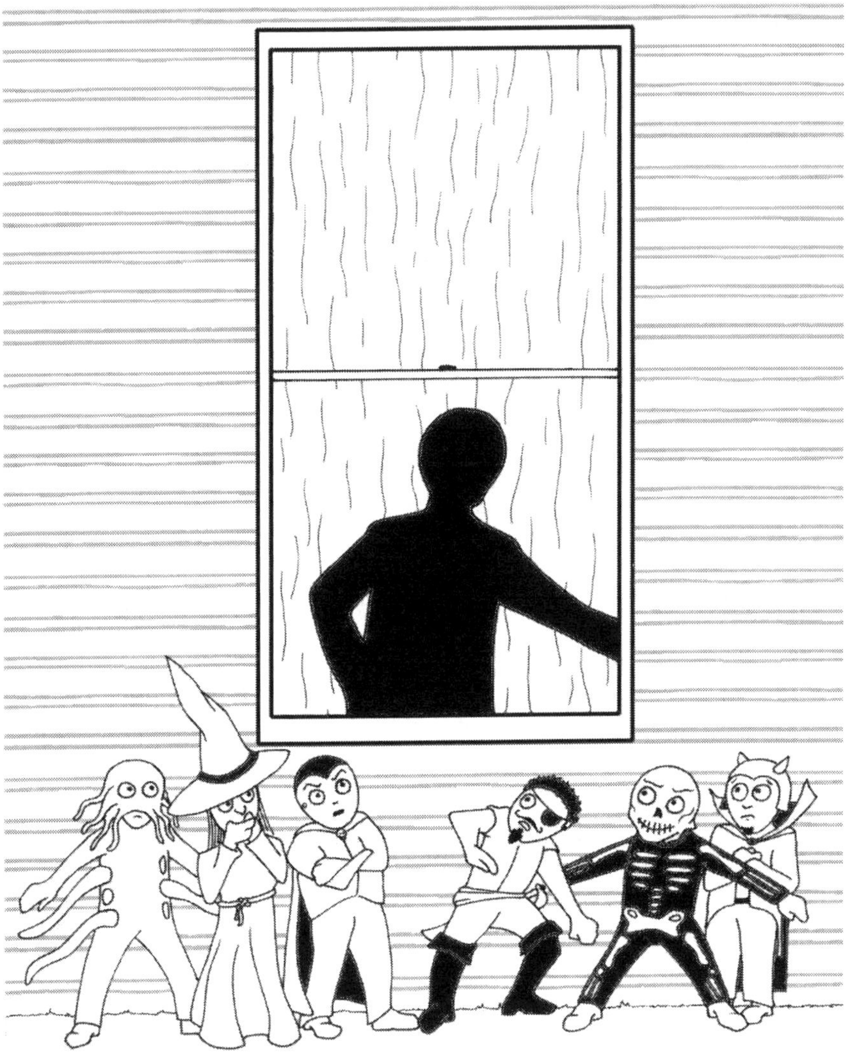

tears from his face with his eyepatch.

"Let's get outta here," said Bobby, and they moved quickly in among the tombstones.

"Next year?" asked the pirate as he adjusted his plastic sword and pulled a caramel from his candy sack.

They all nodded in assent, and joyfully dispersed into the night.

~

The skeleton lagged and at last vanished into the yews. Tomorrow the children would secrete themselves about the graves and giggle as the little old man would grumble and clean his yard, his porch—scrub his windows—re-secure his spouting. They would chuckle carefully, quietly—under their breath. But theirs would not be the only careful, quiet, under-the-breath chuckles, thought the skeleton. He who had given them the night's best treat would be carefully chuckling, too. He was, in fact, chuckling now.

The best treat was always no treat at all, and all the aftermath accompanying such a rudeness. The schemes and plotting pursuant to avenging one's self against those who offered no goodies far outweighed all candies as the most wondrous treat. He could never pass up the chance of offering such a treat.

True, new tactics would be required next year to petrify that chubby vampire, but even this year he had outdone himself. The timer light and the cardboard silhouette propped between the lamp and the window had been his best touch yet.

Oh, for that tremor of chilling blood once more. The exhilaration of being young and afraid again. But enough of such musings. Youth had long since fled, and fear was now a faraway tingling only tasted through puerile, untainted surrogates.

It was no matter. As he unlocked the cottage door, the little skeleton pushed his mask to one side to better scratch at the fluffy gray whiskers beneath.

THE HAIRY MAN
BY JULIA BENALLY

It was time to hunt again. Jay hadn't gotten anything that morning, but he was sure he would this evening. All that hiking through stickers, up mountains, freezing and exhausted while lugging a 30-30 on his shoulder, couldn't be for nothing. Now all he had to do was make sure no one from work recognized him, because he had called in sick so he could hunt.

"You're gonna get your elk today," he told himself as he walked to his room and slipped on his hiking boots. Jay was a tall, wiry man in his early twenties with short, black hair. His handsome face was clear, devoid of the damaging signs of a drinker. Jay possessed the ideal features of an Apache: chiseled, square jaw, high cheek bones and twinkling black eyes. There wasn't a lazy bone in his body.

Just then his sixteen-year-old-brother Derry poked his head in, sneaky-like.

"Jay," he whispered, "you almost ready?"

Derry sported a pudgy belly. His silky hair fell low over his forehead and down his neck. He was the shortest joker in his class, in the entire high school, actually. The girls said he smelled and he couldn't play basketball, but he could tear up Metal Gear like a boss.

"Don't look like you're sneaking," Jay said. "May will see you!"

Jay and Derry did not want their eight-year-old niece to come. She would do nothing but complain she was tired, hungry and then she would have to go to the bathroom. That would mean one of them would have to supervise her, which meant postponing the hunt until she was good and ready. Besides, they didn't take little girls to the bathroom. It was indecent.

"Go out and act natural-like," Jay advised Derry. "Where is she anyway?"

No sooner did he ask than a pink clad girl kicked the door open and jumped into the room. Her black, braided hair was in a royal mess, smashed beneath a pink fishing hat. She was neither a stick nor a ball, but somewhere in between. She boasted a pair of black-rimmed glasses with a tiny sticker of Kirby on one side.

"I'm ready!" May announced as she brandished a two-foot hunting knife with a wicked curve. "Let's kill!"

Derry jumped back.

"Put that away before you chop off Derry's balls," Jay said.

"Hey!" Derry glared at Jay.

"I'll be in the car!" May sped from the room. No one was going to make her stay.

"Don't worry," said Derry, "I'll throw her out." And he marched after her.

Jay didn't reply. May was in the car and that's where she was going to stay no matter what anyone said. He could probably just not go and creep away later, but then it would be too late. With an exasperated sigh, he donned his hunting orange—a flimsy vest that would keep him safe from being shot by other hunters.

Finished dressing, he headed out to his car. It was a simple four-door. It used to be blue. Jay wished he had a truck, but all he had was this half broken rez ride, meaning a junky trashcan of a vehicle full of pop cans and wrappers, same as his fellow Apaches drove. The cars always broke down and they usually smelled. A rez ride would be a thing of the past in a few months, though. Jay was saving up for a Dodge Ram. He wouldn't ask Sara to marry him until he had that beautiful piece of finery. It just wouldn't do to let a bride ride in a slop house on wheels.

Right now, Derry was just standing outside of it yelling at May, "Get out right now!"

"Never!" May held up a knife defiantly. "Come any closer and I'll skewer you right through that pop belly!"

Derry gritted his teeth. "You can't come!"

"Yes, I can," May said. "And I'll tell Jay's boss where he is, too, if I can't come!"

Jay went livid. "You little brat! I'll make you hike all over the place until you're crying!"

"I bet I won't cry," May said smugly as an awful grin

spread over her face.

Jay's eyes turned to slits. "Let's see you not cry then. Hold my gun, don't bump the scope and don't drink anything while you're holding it!" And he shoved the gun at May who propped it up so the barrel was aiming at the roof.

Derry retained his gun. He was quite sure May was going to pour something down the barrel.

"Get in the car, Derry," Jay growled, and then they were off.

"When is Grant coming home?" Derry asked, referring to their older brother, who was May's father. "He can take a belt to May's butt."

"He'll take it to yours when he finds out you were lying to me about hunting," May said.

"Shut up already," Jay snarled, hoping May would get lost in the woods.

The hunting grounds were about fifteen minutes away on one of the many dirt roads that branched off from the highway and into the forest. The pine trees were always green, but the lush vegetation of summer was gone, leaving the forest floor a brown carpet of dead needles and patches of white grass. The sticker bushes were thriving.

Jay parked the car off the dirt road next to a mountain. It was almost evening already and the hunt would be rather short. Still, Jay was determined to make May hike all that annoying energy out so that tomorrow she wouldn't want to go. He doubted they would see anything, let alone be able to shoot something. May was just so pink and loud.

"Give me my gun," Jay said to her before glancing at his brother. "Derry... Derry?"

Derry was slumped in his seat, fast asleep.

May rolled her eyes and smacked Derry in the head. "Hey, Booty Brain, it's time to go!" She jumped out of the car and slammed the door, breathing deeply of the fall air. Her breath smoked heavily before her face and floated away like a miniature ghost.

At last, Derry jerked out of his doze.

Jay rolled his eyes. "What are you doing asleep?" he asked. "May is ready to go before you!" He straightened up and tried to decide how they would conduct this hunt now that May was here, when all of a sudden, she zipped to his side.

"I'm going with you, Jay," she said. "I have to tell you about the new story I made up about Kirby!"

"You're not supposed to talk at all," responded Jay in some horror. He had heard enough of that pink, gumball-looking thing to last him at least six lifetimes. It was disgusting that May always wore pink because Kirby was her hero. "You'll chase all the elk away, so *whisper* if you have to say something."

"Okay," May whispered almost inaudibly. She bent low and scanned the shady forest around her. Although there were a lot of sticker bushes here, the area seemed strangely clear. The pines were spaced equally apart as if they had been planted. She could see far back among the trees. "I want to see you kill something, Jay! Derry can't even aim his pee in the toilet."

Jay snorted as Derry stumbled out of the car.

"What?" he asked.

"You and May hike up this side. I'm going around to the other side."

Derry glared at May as if she were a maggot. "I'm not going with her!"

"Derry's a butt," May said indignantly.

"You wanted to come, you do as I say," Jay barked. "Shut up, Derry. May will keep you awake!"

"Man," Derry grumbled and started walking swiftly up the hill. May ran after him as Jay got back in the car, placed his gun in the front seat and drove to the other side of the mountain. Hopefully, Derry and May would spook the elk and make them come to him.

Meanwhile, Derry was practically running up the mountain, hoping to torture May. The little girl was right behind him, gasping and dripping with sweat, but she was determined to keep up. She didn't know why Derry was hurrying. He looked ready to faint. They reached the top of the mountain in a few minutes.

"Well," Derry gasped, bending over and holding his belly, "the elk are probably to Jay now. Don't get grossed out and start crying when you see the blood all over the place. The elk sometimes don't die right away and... they cry." It was a vindictive little tirade, meant to teach the little brat not to mess with man stuff.

"I'll catch you when *you* faint, Derry," May said.

Derry glared at her. "Can you keep up with me going down?" he said with tight lips. It was more a challenge than a question. "It's really steep. I'm not catching you if you fall."

He marched away like he was Mangus Colorado himself. May ran after him like a tiny demon. Derry was purposely taking the biggest strides that he could. He kept his proud, manly head straight up and refused to look where he was going. The mountain side was as slippery and steep as Derry had said, but he galloped down it like an expert. May scrambled determinedly after him, grabbing fiercely onto sticks and branches to keep from falling. Derry was rapidly pulling away from her and the sun was going down. Nevertheless, May continued on at her slower pace, eying his retreating form with scorn.

"You better hurry up, May," Derry sang out to her. "Bigfoot might be up here looking for little brats!" He chuckled and then he tripped. He was going so fast that he couldn't steady himself. With a startled cry, he flew forward head first and tumbled down the mountain. He sounded like a charging bear, but he was squeaking in pain all the way down instead of growling.

May sat down laughing, slapping her knees in ecstasy. She heard Jay somewhere down below start shouting, but the air was echoing too much for her to hear what he was saying. Finally, she heard her uncle calling her name, and then she spotted him hiking up to her. A small smile creased his lips.

"Come on," he said. "Derry jacked himself up." He started chuckling. "We have to go home now." He pulled her up and they carefully descended the rest of the way.

The afterglow lay like a blush on the trees by the time they got to the bottom. Derry was sitting on the hood gingerly nursing his wounds. When May saw him, she busted out laughing again.

"I almost lost all my posterity and you're laughing," Derry moaned.

May just laughed all the harder as Jay smacked him with his hat.

"Get in the car," Jay growled. "If you can sit." He hid a smirk as he got in and started the engine. Just then, four giant bull elk ran across the road.

"Look!" May squeaked from the back seat.

The beasts halted at the sound of her boisterous voice and stared at them. Jay's eyes widened in surprise. Where had these come from?! Forgetting to stuff his ears in the excitement, he rolled down the glass, leaned his gun on the windowsill and took aim at the lungs of the biggest bull. He pulled the trigger and everything went silent as Jay went temporarily deaf. He didn't even hear his gun go off, it was so loud. Did he even hit it? Derry's mouth moved silently as May leaped out of the car and ran after the elk with Derry on her heels.

"Wait!" Jay shouted, still unable to hear himself. His brother and niece didn't seem to hear him, either. He made sure his tag was still in his pocket as he jumped out of the car and raced after the pair.

By the time he caught up to them, he could hear his own breath and the pine needles crunching under his hiking boots again.

"You got it, you got it!" May jumped up and down. The giant bull was crumpled in a huge heap. Not far away his fellow bulls stared. They knew they were safe from the hunters now.

"It's a seven by seven," Derry said before pulling May back. "Don't go near it, May. Wait for it to be dead."

Their squabble had melted in the joy of the kill.

Jay smiled. "One of us has to stay here and guard the elk and the other one can go get Jimmy."

Jimmy had a working truck and a group of guys at his command to help gut and quarter the elk.

"I'll get him," Derry volunteered.

"I wanna stay with you, Jay," said May.

"No," said Jay as he peered closer at the horns. "You go home and get warm."

"But I am warm."

"It's going to get really cold."

"But I have to see!" May whined desperately as she removed her hat. "I hunted for it and I'm the one who saw it! Please, please, please let me stay! I want to see you gut the elk!"

Jay glanced at his kill and then at May who looked so hopeful. He didn't feel like she was much of a brat anymore. "Alright, but you go with Derry to get Jimmy. You can come back."

"Yes!" May burst out and skipped back to the car.

Derry hurried after May. He was looking pretty happy as well, considering his condition. Jay glanced back at the bull, waiting for it to stop twitching, when Derry shouted, "Jay, the car won't move!"

This couldn't be happening, Jay thought. They were out in the middle of the forest and it was almost night. Turning around, he headed back to the road. Derry was vainly pumping the gas pedal whilst May swigged Dr. Pepper nonchalantly in the backseat.

"So," she said, "are we walking home?"

Jay glanced at the deepening shadows. The trees looked like madmen with wild hair reaching maniacally to the evening sky.

"Derry," he said, "open the hood, and give me the flashlight."

Derry obeyed with some alacrity. He didn't like the dark. As Jay propped the hood open, something putrid wafted on the slight breeze. It wasn't rotting, yet it pierced his senses like a gas burning his brain. Where had it come from? Why hadn't he smelled it before? It jerked the tears from his eyes and made it hard to inhale. It tasted like sour sewer on his tongue. Wiping his face, he gazed in the direction the wind was coming from. Something stood very straight about three hundred feet behind the car. It was tall and black like the trees. Jay's heart seized up.

"Derry," he whispered, hoping May wouldn't suspect

anything. "Derry!"

"What?" Derry asked.

"Come here."

The sound in Jay's voice made Derry unusually sensible, and he got out of the car, shutting the door behind him.

"What is that?" Jay nodded imperceptibly in the direction of the figure.

Derry turned his head, and a small gasp escaped his lips. "Is it a man?"

"It's too tall to be a man."

"I-It's probably just a tree," Derry said.

Jay handed his brother the flashlight and quickly began checking the fluids in the car. The light in Derry's hand started to shake.

"Hurry, Jay," he whispered.

The sun was already behind the mountains and the afterglow was gone. A cold blue lay on the world. The wind washed like freezing fingers over the pair.

"You find anything?" Derry asked after awhile.

The transmission fluid had leaked out. Jay glanced at the trunk of the car, where he had an extra container of fluid, and then at the figure against the trees. It seemed to be closer and bigger.

"It's just the shadows, Jay," he whispered to himself, walking as calmly as possible to the trunk. He kept his eyes on the hulking figure, afraid to turn his back on it.

Just as he did so, Derry suddenly released a gasping whimper.

"It's walking to us!" he half sobbed, scrambling for his gun in the front seat. Jay glanced back and sprinted for the passenger door. He could see the figure striding effortlessly towards him.

"What is it?" May turned around and tried to look out the back window, but her uncle hadn't closed the trunk in his panic and it blocked her view.

Jay wrenched the door open just as Derry took aim at the creature. It was then that Jay realized what Derry was about to do.

"Derry, don't!" he shouted, but it was too late: Derry fired.

The thing collapsed on the spot without making a single sound. May flung her door open and tried to get out, but Jay shoved her back inside.

"Don't move!" he snapped. Mustering all the courage he had, he scrambled back to the trunk and yanked out the bottle of transmission fluid. He slammed the trunk door down as Derry demanded in a shaking voice, "Is it dead?!"

Jay didn't answer as he poured the fluid recklessly into the car.

"J-Jay!" Derry suddenly yelped.

Jay looked to where the thing had fallen, and his heart went into his mouth. It was *getting up*. His breath grew short as he tossed the empty bottle to the side and began screwing the cap back on as fast as he could. The thing was on its feet just as Jay dropped the hood. Derry jumped behind the wheel. The thing broke into a run straight for them.

Screaming, Derry started the car up. Jay dove into the passenger's seat just in time before Derry could leave him behind.

"May!" Jay searched wildly in the back for her.

"Here," May whispered from behind Derry's seat. She was curled into a ball on the floor with her jacket over her head.

The car bounced and scraped over rocks and deep ruts in the road.

"Derry, careful!" Jay cried.

His brother didn't answer. The gas pedal was floored, and Derry's knuckles were white. The dirt plumed out from under the wheels like brown mist veiled in the car's red back lights. Knowing that Derry could very well crash, Jay moved to buckle in his seat belt. That was when he heard grunting just outside the car, like a huge, bloody heart drumming from a rough throat.

"What's that noise?!" May asked.

Out of the corner of his eye, Jay spotted the hairy figure racing beside his window. It reached for the door handle. With a horrified gasp, Jay quickly popped his lock down and the hairy man jiggled the handle in vain. It reached for the back door's handle and Jay smacked that lock down too, just in time.

"May, lock your door!" Jay shouted.

May obeyed without question, never revealing her head from under the jacket.

Great, hairy hands batted at the windows and it tried to

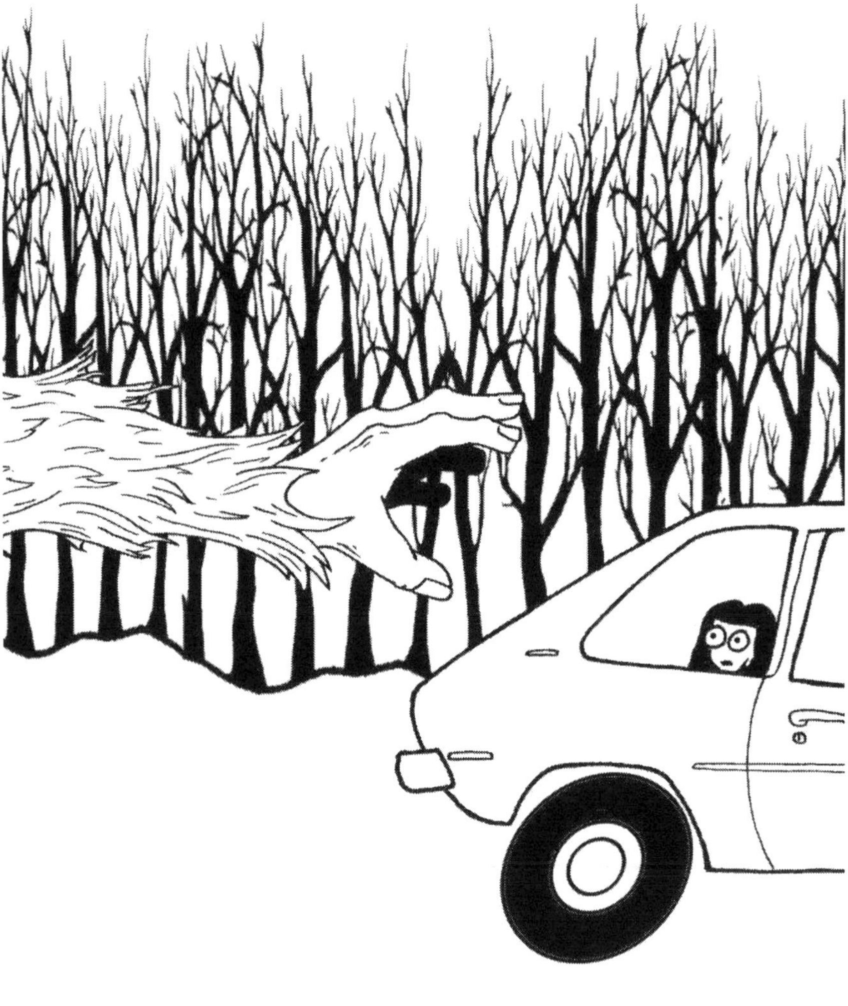

make eye contact through the glass. Jay covered his face as Derry hunched over, his shoulders blocking his side view. Suddenly, one of the huge hands slammed on the windshield. The hand could have wrapped around their heads, and it was covered in matted, filthy fur. With an awful screech, Derry veered the car into the creature. The entire vehicle shuddered and skidded this way and that over the massive rocks lying in the gutter. The bottom scraped on an unusually large stone with sharp points.

"I got it," Derry voiced with a relieved gasp.

Derry drove like a madman back to town. For a few minutes, it seemed that they would be okay, but the car went slower and slower no matter what Derry did.

"Jay, what's happening?!" Derry wailed in alarm. The entire car shuddered and then just stopped. They were a mile from town.

"What'll we do, what'll we do?!" Derry moaned as he pressed vainly on the gas pedal.

"Shut up," Jay growled. "The phone's in range again." He flipped his cell open and dialed his dad. He didn't dare call Grant because Grant would kill him for putting May in danger. Immediately a woman's annoying, automated voice sounded: *"You have insufficient minutes to make this call."*

"What's she talkin' about?" Jay asked. "It says I have no minutes!"

Derry was very quiet, but May spoke up, "Derry let his girlfriend use your phone to call her friend in California."

"WHAT?!" Jay exploded as Derry sank low in his seat.

"And her face was all greasy," May added.

Jay seized Derry roughly by the shirt, his fist ready to pound him, when he realized May was still in the car. She stared with big eyes.

"We have to walk," said Jay shortly, shoving Derry against the window like so much refuse.

"I..." Derry began.

"Shut up!" Jay barked. "May, let's go."

"But that thing is out there," Derry said.

Jay didn't answer as he got out and took May firmly by the hand. Flicking on the flashlight, he walked swiftly away. Derry watched a few seconds before realizing the hairy man might come to the car while he was in it. Hurrying out, he left his door wide open and scurried after the pair.

The moon had not yet risen and the inky dark concealed their surroundings. It was so quiet and eerie. No cars would be driving by on the dirt road anytime soon. Jay walked so fast that May had to run to keep up. Derry remained close, almost clutching Jay's arm, but not daring to. The single shaft of light lit the road ahead. Every few seconds, Jay shined the light warily into the forest. Every pass over the trees the trio expected to see the hairy man.

"Jay." May clutched his arm in terror. "I hear something."

"I-I don't hear anything," Derry stammered, trying to block out the sound of a fourth pair of footfalls behind them.

"Keep walking, May. Just look at the road, okay?" Jay sniffed the cold air for the rancid stench of the monster, but nothing. The wind was blowing into their faces.

"My legs hurt," May whispered.

Jay knelt on the ground. "Get on my back."

"No," May whimpered. "It might get me if I'm on your back!"

"I'll hold you then," Jay said, shuddering at the thought of the hairy man that close. As he lifted her up, May glanced at the blackness behind them and gasped in horror. There was a pair of glowing, scarlet eyes several heads taller than Jay.

"It's here!" May shouted as she started to cry.

Without another word, Jay and Derry sprinted up the road. Just as the town lights twinkled through the trees, they heard heavy footfalls behind them. They were a distance away at first, but growing louder as they gained. The dogs started yowling in terror as if a bear had walked into town. May buried her face in Jay's neck, every second expecting the hairy hands to grasp her uncle and drag him back. She could hear her uncles gasping, and several feet away she heard the heavy breathing of the hairy man. Deep down she knew that he was angry at them because Derry had shot him. Why was he always doing something stupid? Everyone knew that you were never supposed to shoot the hairy man! Even the kindergarteners knew that!

A few seconds more and Jay and Derry spotted an old house right on the edge of the forest. A single orange streetlight lit their way. Fear and hope of escape injected strength into their aching legs. Never before had they run so fast so far. As their feet crunched over dead leaves and dry sticks, the dark seemed to gape like an open maw behind them, echoing with the dirge of that bloody heartbeat. At last they stumbled onto the little back porch, and Jay pounded on the door as hard as he could. The wailing of the dogs grew louder and louder; ghosts screeching from the very pits of their unmarked tombs beneath the town.

"Let us in," Derry screamed. "It's coming, it's coming!"

No one opened the door.

Suddenly, an empty, despairing wail cut through the crying dogs like a burning knife, piercing their ears. And then, abrupt silence. The trio froze where they stood, huddled against the door, the air in their lungs sharp and quick. Their hearts hammered against their chests and pounded in their ears. Only one thought passed through their terrified minds: the door would not open.

There seemed to be something standing just beyond the circle of orange. A fog swirled from a certain point in the black and into the light. May clutched Jay's neck so tight he could hardly breathe. His own strained breath smoked away from him, just like that fog in the light. And then the hairy man stepped into view. The black hair nearly covered a savage, cruel face. The red eyes glinted with hatred. An ugly grin spread over that gnarled visage that smoked with thick breath. Without warning, it darted forward with more speed than it had shown before. The three shrieked in terror, and then the door opened. They tumbled in a heap on the floor as an old man shouted at them to get out of the way. He couldn't close the door.

The hairy man leaped onto the porch in a low crouch, eyes burning like magma, as its would-be victims scrambled madly back. It took another leap and the old man slammed the door shut in its face. The old wood shuddered on impact and bent inward. Quick as a wink, the old man locked the door tight just before the knob jiggled violently.

Thud-thud-thud went its heavy steps as it loped swiftly around the house. The bloody heartbeat drummed. The frail, wooden structure vibrated. Every knob in the house went *chick-chick-chick!* The windows strained and every awful second they expected to hear glass shatter, or a door creak open to let in the freezing autumn air. The four stood very still, their eyes following the din of the hairy man round and round the house.

It wasn't until around 8:00 that the sounds gave way to crying dogs. Fainter and fainter the wails grew until they, too, fell silent once more. It was the quiet of safety. The monster had finally gone.

"Jay," said the old man softly, "I'll drive you home."

Jay finally realized that they were in Jimmy's house. Very stealthily, the old man led them back out into the night and stuffed them into his truck. The three glanced furtively out the windows at the houses and streetlights as Jimmy conveyed them carefully back home. No breath stirred. Not a single person poked their heads out; no light escaped the tightly closed curtains.

A few minutes later, their rescuer pulled into their

driveway. To their utter relief, they recognized Grant's car. May's mom and dad were home at last. A well of relief hit Jay like a wave and he nearly broke down in tears. Without even a word of thanks, Derry and May dashed into the house as fast as they could.

"Jay," said Jimmy as he got out, "you better stay out of the woods for awhile."

"Yeah," Jay responded, glancing warily around. "Thanks for the ride, Jimmy."

"No problem."

Jay closed the door and sped into the house. May was already telling her parents about the terrifying events from the safety of her mother's gentle arms. Jay made sure the front door was properly locked.

"Jay," said Grant sternly as he removed Derry's hat. The boy was in palpitations on the couch. "You alright?"

Jay rubbed the back of his neck. "I... I think I'm just going to work tomorrow." And with that, he went straight to the shower. Turning the hot water on, he let it wash away the sweat and the grime. The sound of the running water drowned out the night terrors and the dogs that once more took up their wailing somewhere by Jimmy's house.

THE TRIPLE DARE
BY MIRACLE AUSTIN

My so-called best friend didn't believe me when I confessed what I saw that Halloween night, but maybe you will...

~

Howling winds ushered in Hallow's Eve at fifty-eight degrees—odd for Truth, Texas since the temperatures usually peaked in the high nineties that time of year. The leaves on the trees transformed almost overnight into spicy bright auburns, sunflower yellows, popping lime greens, and dark coffee browns.

Goosebumps ran up and down my arms as I walked downtown to Fancy's Costume World with my bestie Jezene. The whole way there, I swear I heard someone whispering incoherent, raspy words in my ears.

In the sardine-can-sized dressing room, I tried on costume after costume, but once I donned a blue shredded knee-length dress and white apron, I knew that was it. I would be Alice in Wonderland, but with a zombie twist. I twirled around and stared at myself in the tall, antique dressing mirror with two silver gargoyles planted on each side. Their onyx eyes were gigantic and piercing, and I felt as if they were staring right through me.

Jezene was at the front of the store, trying on different monster masks as I scooped up some zombie make-up and prosthetics. In line, I met Mr. Tatter, my sixth grade science teacher. He was one of the cool ones and always so easy to talk to. He would roll up his sleeves on special occasions and show us his crazy tattoos, which practically painted his arms from shoulder to wrist. There was an odd clown design that always intrigued me. I wish I could've cloned him for high school too.

"Great costume, Sharmin," he said. "You should wear it to my annual Hallow's Eve party tonight. Why don't you and your friend drop by? I'm making my famous brownies with both dark and white chocolate."

A huge smile appeared on my face like the Cheshire Cat. "Oh, I loved those when you brought them to class. Can't believe how long it's been since I've seen you, Mr. Tatter."

"Yes, that's the thing with time—it never stops but is a perpetual beast." Mr. Tatter finished paying and tipped his blue fedora toward me. "Always a pleasure, Ms. Knight. I hope to see you tonight."

"Happy Hallow's Eve," I said.

Jezene and I exited the store with bags tied around our waist. The sun was diving down faster that night, as if someone had tossed a lasso around it to tug it down, and the brisk winds felt like cat scratches on my bare face.

"Mr. Tatter invited us to his annual Hallow's Eve party," I said. "Wanna go?"

"Not really, Sharmin." Jezene smirked as she dug out a neon blue lipstick from her backpack to paint her dry pursed lips. "But if you wanna go, then go. Everyone knows that you were Mr. Tatter's favorite."

"Whatever. I just completed my assignments on time."

"So did I," she said. "For the science project, I even glued the title on the top of the board and tossed glitter to give it something. Mr. Tatter still gave me an F-minus."

"Good grief, Jezene. Just let it go."

We separated from each other and waved goodbye. I lived about three more blocks down, so I walked faster to get out of the cold. Mr. Tatter's house was on my way. He always decorated it with Halloween flare—purple, white, and orange blinking lights made it the best-decorated place in town. I stopped in front of his porch and stood there in an almost trance-like state, staring at the decorations. A few younger kids ran up to the bright door with glittery cobwebs hanging in the corners. Mr. Tatter answered and invited them in. Then he saw me on the sidewalk.

"Sharmin, great to see you again," he said as he approached me. "Where's Jezene?"

I was speechless for a moment.

"She's tied up," I said. "I wanted to at least stop by for a minute."

"Well, come on in for a little bit, at least to get warm. I'll fix you some cocoa with a brownie, fresh out of the oven."

He placed his hand on my shoulder. "You're shivering."

A sharp chill shot through my fingers all the way down to my toes. I suddenly wanted to be far from this place.

"Thank you, Mr. Tatter," I said. "Sounds tempting, but I'd better get home. My mom is a worrywart."

"You can call her. I'll vouch for you." His hand remained.

I backed up. "Oh, that's okay. Thanks anyway."

"I understand," he said. "If you happen to change your mind, then come on back."

"Bye, Mr. Tatter." I turned around and started jogging toward my house. I looked back once and saw Mr. Tatter still standing in the same position that I left him with a weird smirk planted on his face. I felt as if he was staring right through me like the gargoyles in the costume shop.

At home, I locked both bolts behind me. Before I could pull the curtains shut, a warm hand grazed my neck.

I jumped. "Jeez! Let me know you're in the room, ninja-mom."

"Gosh honey, I didn't mean to startle you." She brushed back her ebony hair and reached out to touch my hands. "You're freezing. Sit down. I'll make us some warm chamomile tea with honey and ginger."

At the table, I stared toward the window.

"You okay?" she asked.

"Yeah, I'm fine. You just gave me the heebie-jeebies."

Mr. Tatter gave me the heebie-jeebies too, but I didn't want to mention him around Mom. She already didn't like him and never supported me going to those parties of his. *One of the strangest birds I've ever met*, she'd always said.

She walked over with the warm tea simmering in purple jack-o-lantern-shaped coffee cups. Then she sat down, scooted her chair over to me and gave me a hug.

I smiled. "What's that for?"

"I just love you so much and never want you to forget that."

"Love you too, Mom," I said and held my warm cup in both hands. "Hey, don't forget that I'm hanging out with Jezene tomorrow night."

"Oh, that Halloween party in the woods?" She shook her head. "Sharmin, I really wish you would change your mind and stay in with me instead. We could fix popcorn on the stove, make s'mores, and watch black-and-white scary movies all night."

"Mom," I whined, "you know Jezene and I attend this party every year. Plus it's chaperoned by several parents from school."

She placed her teacup down. "I just worry about you. You know I was watching a news special tonight about the Hallow's Eve Serial Killer. He's murdered dozens of people, mostly teens."

"Why do you watch creepy shows like that? You always end up having nightmares."

She sighed. "Just stay away from No Man's Land, okay?"

At the mention of that place, the hair on the back of my neck stood up. "Why would I go out there?"

"I don't know, honey, but just don't, okay?"

"I promise, Mom." I hugged her again, tighter this time. "And don't worry about that serial killer. I'm sure he's nowhere around Truth."

~

The next day, with Mom's help, I slipped on the long, blonde knotted-up wig with puffy bangs and painted my eyes with glittery, smoky eye shadow. The make-up balanced well with my caramel skin. After Mom glued fake zombie scars on my cheeks, forehead, and forearms, I stepped into my costume and twirled around in the bathroom mirror. Not only did I look pretty darn hot, but I was pretty scary too.

Jezene arrived, dressed up in a 1920's costume—a short red fringe dress, long black gloves kissing her elbows, and a strand of white pearls adorning her neck. A black, sparkly headband with a red feather pinned on its side hugged her short purple bob nicely.

I smiled. "Wow, you've really outdone yourself."

"I already know I look great," Jezene said, switching her mouth like a rabbit, while adjusting her purple fangs with her pierced tongue. "You look *okay*, Sharmin. Let's go already."

"Hold on," I said and snuck back into my bedroom to slip on my unicorn locket. It didn't really match the costume, but I wanted to wear it anyway. It was the last Christmas gift that my dad gave me. Before he went to No Man's Land and never came back.

As Jezene and I headed down the highway in her SUV, she pulled a cigarette out of her purse and lit it up.

I started coughing and pushed the button to let the window down.

"Seriously, Sharmin, it's freezing! Let it up."

"Put the poison out first," I said. "And I thought you stopped your nasty little habit."

"Guess you thought wrong." She shook her head and blew smoke out the side of her mouth like a pro. "Anyway, I'm just nervous."

"Nervous about what? We do this every year."

"Yeah, I guess. But I heard Link Chambers might show up."

"Really?" My heartbeat started running laps around the track.

"Yep." Jezene smiled as she took another puff and threw the cigarette out.

On the gravel road where the party was held every year, tall lit Halloween ghosts and jack-o-lanterns guided our path. We could hear popular dance music blasting from the multiple standing speakers posted all around.

It looked like all of Truth High was accounted for. Snacks and Halloween desserts flooded the tables with huge bowls of orange and black fruit punch at both ends. This was definitely the place to be tonight.

After an hour of dancing, a group gathered around a huge campfire. We all sat on long logs. Stacy Hines, a senior and probably the prettiest girl at Truth High, looked all around to make sure the adults weren't monitoring and whispered, "Who wants to really turn this party up with Truth or Dare?"

Everyone nodded except me. I just shook my head and started to stand up.

"Come on Sharmin," Jezene said, attempting to pull me back down next to her. "It'll be fun."

Then I saw you-know-who walking towards me. Link... Oh, he had amazing ocean-blue eyes and dark curly hair with the perfect mini-Mohawk haircut. He was tall and lean. His cherry sweater stuck to his heaving and well-defined six-pack.

"Hey, Sharmin. What's up?"

Someone must have slipped super glue into my green apple lip-gloss. I couldn't talk, not until Jezene jabbed her finger into my lower leg.

"Ouch!" I yelped.

She leaned forward. "Hey, Link."

He brushed some loose hair out of my eyes. "Awesome costume," he said to me. "You're not leaving, right?'

"No way," I said. "Psyched about Truth or Dare."

He sat next to me. I was about to pee in my pants and scream at the same time.

Jezene rolled her eyes and scooted away from us. Before I could ask what was wrong, the game started.

Easy rounds came first, mostly truths. I answered one or two. They were harmless, until Jezene whispered, "I bet you won't take a dare, Sharmin."

"What? Yeah, I would." My lips trembled and my knees knocked against each other before getting locked up.

"Okay, prove it. I got a really good dare." She stood up and placed her hands on her hips, staring down at me like a predator about to devour her prey. "Sharmin, truth or dare? Oh, wait double dare. No, triple dare?"

Everyone's mouths dropped as they stared at each other. They knew what this meant: the worst dare that could possibly be conjured up.

I looked around at their mouths still frozen open. "Triple Dare!" I shouted.

Jezene rolled her tongue around her mouth and cleared her throat. "I triple dare you to travel down to No Man's Land."

My heart started speeding faster than two racecars about to cross the finish line. I looked at her, tears about to well in my eyes, but I fought them off because Link was right there.

Her dare shocked me. She knew my dad committed suicide there.

"I'm down, Jezene," I said in a crackled tone. I leaned toward her and whispered, "Can we go over there and talk first?"

She shrugged. "Sure."

We walked a few feet away from the camp.

In my mind, I cut her into tiny pieces and blew her dust in the wind with a snap of my fingers. "You're so wrong for this and you know exactly why. I thought you were my best friend, Jezene."

"That's exactly who I am. I'm trying to help you. Time to face your fears, Sharmin. Plus, it looks like you've won the prize tonight." She motioned to the campfire where Link watched us.

"Prize... You mean, Link? Wait, you have a thing for him too?"

"Whatever, Sharmin, it doesn't matter anymore. Looks like he knows who he wants after all this time." Jezene flung her hands up and walked back to the camp.

I turned, my heart beating faster, and stormed away from the group.

Link ran to catch up with me. "Sharmin, wait. You don't have to do this."

"I need to do this, Link."

"At least let me go with you most of the way and wait for you?"

I smiled and nodded.

We walked in silence for a long time before reaching No Man's Land. There was a dilapidated wire fence and 'Keep Out' signs posted in several spots.

As I hiked my dress up, about to jump over the fence, Link blushed and turned around. I think he saw my lacy pink Supergirl undies. I grinned and giggled.

He held my arm for balance, and I crossed over with ease.

"You sure you don't want me to come with you?"

"I'm sure. Thank you for coming this far with me." I hesitated. "Can I ask you a question? Why are you talking to me tonight? I've seen you in school for years and you've never even noticed me until now."

"Yeah, I know. I've been a complete idiot. Sharmin, I've always thought you were super smart and pretty. I've had a crush on you for awhile."

"What?" My faced turned fifty shades of red. I was never the stick-figure kind of girl. I carried my weight well though, and could do a mean salsa solo and whip into a nae nae any day of the week.

He squeezed my hand before I let go. "I'll be right here waiting for you."

I felt warm, although it was only forty-eight degrees.

The winds picked up, and the tree branches rattled up against the other trees as I walked down the grassy slope. I looked behind me, and Link was already out of sight. The crackled whispers from the dark abyss swarmed around me like bees. It seemed like shadows were fighting in the sky under the full moon.

I finally came to a weathered sign that read, *You're about to enter No Man's Land. Turn around now!* It looked like a kindergarten student wrote it backwards.

Up ahead, I noticed a blue-illuminating campfire. I walked a little closer and saw something strange—a large cauldron with smoke rising from the top. A half-dozen creatures stood around it, each one no more than three-and-a-half feet tall. Their bodies were rounded like penguins with skin that resembled white broken eggshells.

I stooped down fast behind some bushes and a huge

broken oak tree stump before they saw me.

The leader carried a tall wooden staff and wobbled around the fire. They all gathered in a circle around the cauldron and interlocked their hairy hands, which looked like pudgy claws.

The leader placed his staff inside the cauldron and stirred it round and round. Whatever was in there, he jabbed and jabbed at it. The others jumped up and down with a roaring, high-pitched cackle that seemed to burn my ears.

They chanted in a language I didn't know, yet somehow I could understand these words: *Your evil practices shall end this night. We've been watching and waiting to devour you.* Who were they talking to?

Suddenly, an arm popped out of the pot. It had a clown tattoo painted on its skin.

That was when I knew who it was. I heard a faint scream and, realizing it had come from me, I clamped my hands on my mouth. One of the creatures looked in my direction, so I brought myself lower to the ground like a soldier in a heated battle.

But it was too late. The leader with the staff began to wobble faster and closer to me. His eyes gleamed a bright crimson, and his mouth opened up wide to reveal several moving rows of long, jagged black teeth.

I rolled onto my side and balanced myself to stand. Then I tore through the dark forest, scratching my hands and legs, trying to jump over low tree branches while constantly looking behind me.

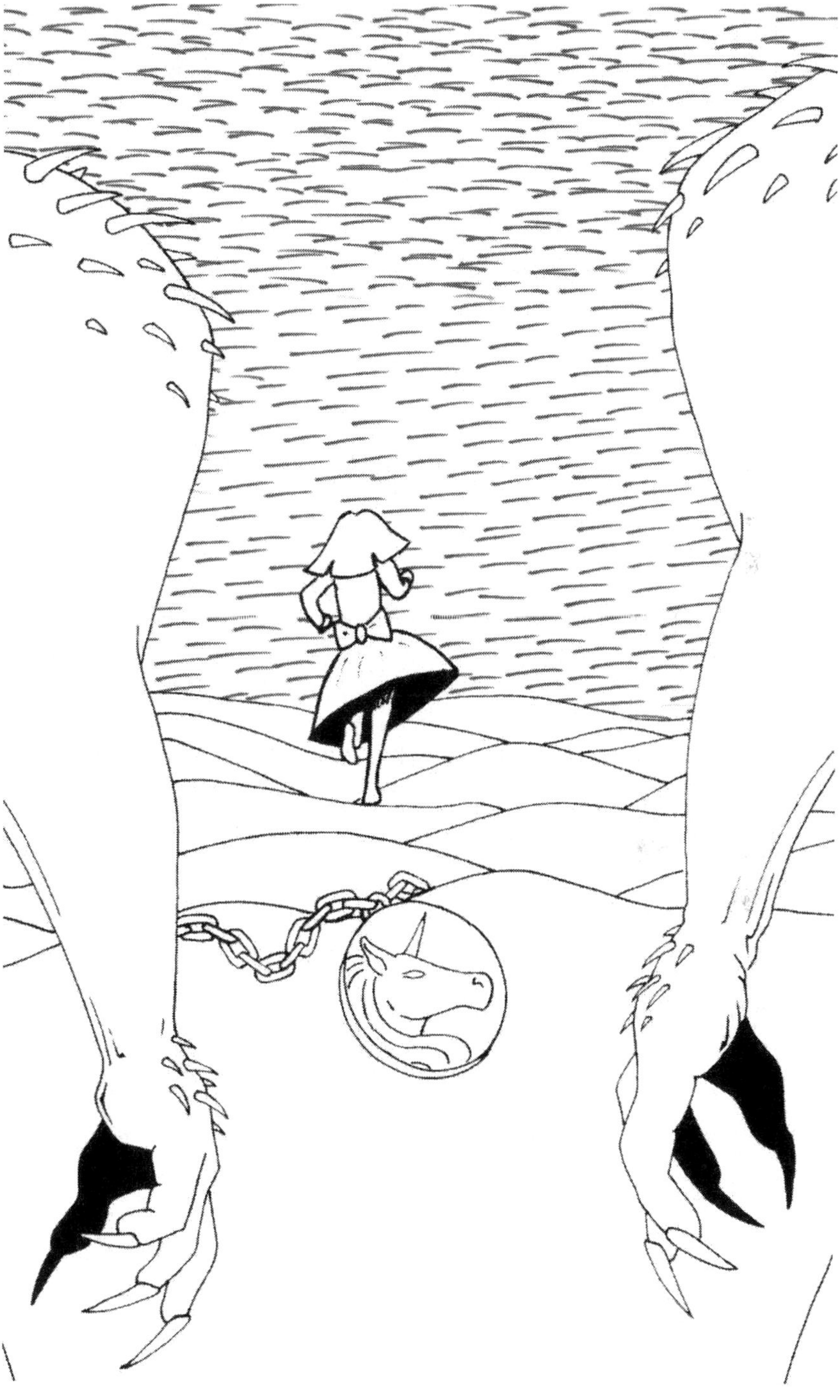

I never saw the leader or his ilk following me.

Out of breath, my dress smeared with mud stains that glistened in the moonlight, I reached Link.

He helped me over the fence. "What in the heck happened to you back there?"

I couldn't talk for several seconds.

"Link, I saw something. I can't explain it."

"Then show me."

"No it's too dangerous; they'll get us."

"Sharmin, it was probably some dumb trick that Jezene is playing on you."

I started thinking maybe he was right, but what I saw looked so real. We walked back into the woods to where I had seen the cauldron and the creatures, but all had vanished.

I stooped to the ground where the campfire had been, but it was cold to touch.

My hand drifted to my neck, and I realized for the first time my unicorn locket was missing. I ran so fast from there I didn't notice it had fallen off. I walked around the area several times in zigzag circles but found nothing.

Link and I walked back to the party. It had started snowing, and a lot of people were already leaving.

I tried to tell Jezene what I'd witnessed, but she denied having anything to do with it.

"Sharmin, you really need help," she said, snickering. "I'm sure you can find your way home."

Link overheard everything and appeared behind me.

"Come on. I'll drive you."

At my house, he walked me to the door and kissed my cheek. "Look, I don't know what you saw tonight, but I want you to know I believe you. I'll come by tomorrow and we can talk more."

I waved goodbye as Link drove off in his truck. Inside, Mom was fast asleep on the sofa. I placed a blanket over her and turned off the lights.

~

The next morning, the news showed footage of Mr. Tatter's home and explained how his basement had over thirty bodies buried there.

A police spokesperson with a deep Texan accent said, "We of Truth, Texas, are both disheartened and shocked that one of our very own, someone we all respected, has now been identified as the Hallow's Eve Serial Killer. The law enforcement here and in several areas around Texas is searching for Mr. Jack Tatter. If you have any information, then please call Truth Police Department or the FBI."

But I already knew they were never going to find him. This would be the first unsolved case for Truth, Texas.

My mom pulled me into her chest and hugged me. "Oh honey, I'm so glad you didn't go to his party."

I wanted to tell her what I had seen last night: the strange creatures and Mr. Tatter in a boiling cauldron. But how could I explain it to her?

I retreated to my bedroom where I found the window open wide, the lemonade-yellow curtains blowing up toward the ceiling like high ocean waves.

Moving forward to lock it, my left foot landed on something cold and round. I bent down to examine what I stepped on. It was my unicorn locket with a message taped around its chain.

It read, *Never mention what you saw at No Man's Land on Halloween. Never or we'll come and get you for our next feast.*

My hands trembled, and the note fell to the ground. It disintegrated into a small pile of ashes.

I never walked near No Man's Land again or spoke of what I witnessed there. Link tried to ask me, but I denied everything.

Things were never the same with Jezene. I sometimes spoke to her in the hall, but never again felt comfortable hanging out with her.

Years later, graduation came and went, and while most of the students at Truth High went their separate ways, Link and I headed off to the Big Apple for college together.

I still have nightmares about that night, although I'm now forty-three years old and married with two teenagers. I haven't been back to Truth in over twenty years. Mom relocated to the East Coast to be near her grandchildren and me. You could say life is pretty good. Well, it is most of the time, minus the nightmares...

Listen to me carefully, okay. I'm not sure why I was able to escape the monsters I saw at No Man's Land that night, but I did. I like to think my late dad's spirit was there and he helped me somehow.

So if you're ever driving through Truth, Texas, on Halloween, then keep on driving until you get to the next city. Don't even think about exploring No Man's Land, even on a dare. Unless of course you want to meet the one with the tall staff and razor teeth.

THE BONES OF HILLSIDE
BY LEE A. FORMAN

The hatch remained hidden and locked in the cellar. Rusty chains and an iron padlock held it down, kept the thing inside from escaping. For years, Robin feared it would break through the rotten wood planks and wondered why it never did. But he gave up thinking about it long ago; all that mattered was that it worked.

He opened the shed to get a rake but gazed past it at the Halloween costume hung on a nail—a black cloak and devil mask. He stared into the empty holes where the eyes of a child would be; emptiness stared back.

He leaned to get the tool, wrapped his fingers around its splintered handle, and retreated, slamming the shed doors behind him. Sweat ran down his brow, and he wiped it with his sleeve. Icicles stabbing at his spine made every part of him shudder. The shed was not a place he favored visiting.

Attempting to clear fallen leaves from the grounds of an entire graveyard with a rake would have been insane, more ludicrous than what his job already entailed. He had a riding mower with a leaf vacuum attachment as well as a leaf blower. But he raked them from graves the old-fashioned way. He did it with care and gently brushed the grass in fine strokes. He couldn't just ride the tractor over their resting places or use the noisy leaf blower. It didn't matter that the coffins contained no remains; he had to respect their memories.

The crunching of leaves diverted Robin's attention, and he looked to see a blue uniform approaching. Cops always rattled his nerves. The thought that they'd find out what he'd been doing repeated itself daily. Handcuffs and a free ride in a police car were never far from his thoughts.

"Good morning," the woman said. "I'm Officer Gabel."

Robin smiled. "Morning. Robin Thomas. What can I do for you?"

"Well, with Halloween coming up I just wanted to check in. You know how the kids are around here."

He let out a forced laugh. "Yeah, I've had to chase them out of here at night many times."

"I know what you mean. It's a busy night for us too. Just be careful and call if you need. We'll be running extra patrols near the cemetery tomorrow night because of what happened last Halloween."

Great, Robin thought. *That's all I need. Cops snooping around here.*

"Thank you, much appreciated," he said. "They did some real damage to the headstones last year."

"They sure did. What kind of person desecrates a grave like that? It makes you wonder... Well, good luck to you.

And happy Halloween."

"You too."

He waited until the uniform went out of sight before going inside to retrieve a beer from the refrigerator. He popped it open and drank quickly, opening another as soon as he emptied the first. With his hand to his chest, he breathed deeply in an attempt to curb the oncoming tremors. He wanted to run, get away from the nightmare, but his conscience tied him there with a tight noose.

After finishing off a six pack, he felt okay enough to go back outside. He peeked through the curtains to ensure no more police had come. He despised the paranoia, but being arrested and locked away seemed insignificant to the consequences that would surely take place after. That's what really terrified him—not jail, not losing his freedom, but the fact that his imprisonment would endanger the lives of innocents.

Moving out into the field of the dead, he started the grim task of choosing which grave to take from. He rubbed his chin and scanned the area, keeping note of which graves he'd already exhumed, so he didn't waste his time digging up an empty coffin. Autumn always entailed extra work—more digging, more bodies, and of course leaving no trace of his extracurricular activities.

The beast's appetite always grew ravenous in October. Something about Halloween riled up the thing living in the hatch, and it took additional meals to keep it satiated. Robin never believed in superstition, but after fifteen years, his outlook on the matter changed. Maybe Halloween was more than just a children's holiday. Maybe it really did have some supernatural significance. Either way, it certainly did in the cursed place he'd been stuck tending to.

"Albert Combs," he read on the headstone. "1935 to 1974. Poor bastard didn't live long." It made him consider his own mortality. Hell, he was nearly pushing 40 already. But he suspected he'd live a long life, cursed to continue on until he joined the ranks he cared for.

Will someone dig me up someday? Will I end up as a meal for that horrible thing?

He waited until nightfall, grudgingly opened the doors to the shed, tried not to look at the devil mask, and retrieved the shovel. He carried it to his chosen site.

"Sorry about this, Albert, but it has to be done."

He stuck the shovel's point into the soft earth and stomped with his boot until it sank in. He pried up the dirt and repeated the process until it felt as though his back would break. The moon waltzed along the sky, and by the time he'd reached bottom, it was nearly dawn. He wiped the last layer of dirt away by hand and stood over the coffin a long time, dreading its opening even though he'd done it countless times before.

"Hey there, Albert. Sorry I have to disturb you like this. But think of the good you'll do. It's an honorable cause." Robin sighed and pried open the lid. "Hope you lived a good life, pal." He tied a rope around Albert's waist and climbed out of the grave. With both feet firmly planted, he hoisted old Albert out and carefully placed him in a wheelbarrow. "Come on. Let's go for a little ride."

He wheeled Albert's decimated remains home and brought him inside. With the body over his shoulder, he took him to the cellar and placed him next to the hatch. It shook violently and the chains clanged against the wood planks. Robin gritted his teeth. He hated what lived in there. He hated that it got excited when it came time to feed. He hated everything about it. Sometimes at night, when he'd be quietly in bed, he thought he could hear it breathing—a raspy, broken rattle that drove him to insomnia.

The hatch had its own smaller door that Robin opened to feed the beast. It didn't have a lock, only a small anchor that held it shut. The creature could never fit through the opening—its sole purpose was for feeding the wretched thing.

"You know, Al? Sometimes I wonder about this thing. Where did it come from? How long has it been here? Probably better not to know."

He gripped his hatchet and got to work separating the bones, starting with the arms and legs, then the torso and spine. Once he'd chopped a nice pile, he started dropping them down the hole one by one. Growls and the crunching of teeth resonated in the dank cellar. The only thing he never sent down was the skull. He figured it best to leave at least some remains intact. Once the feeding ended, he'd write the names and dates of the sacrificed on the skull in permanent marker. He'd accumulated quite a collection over the years.

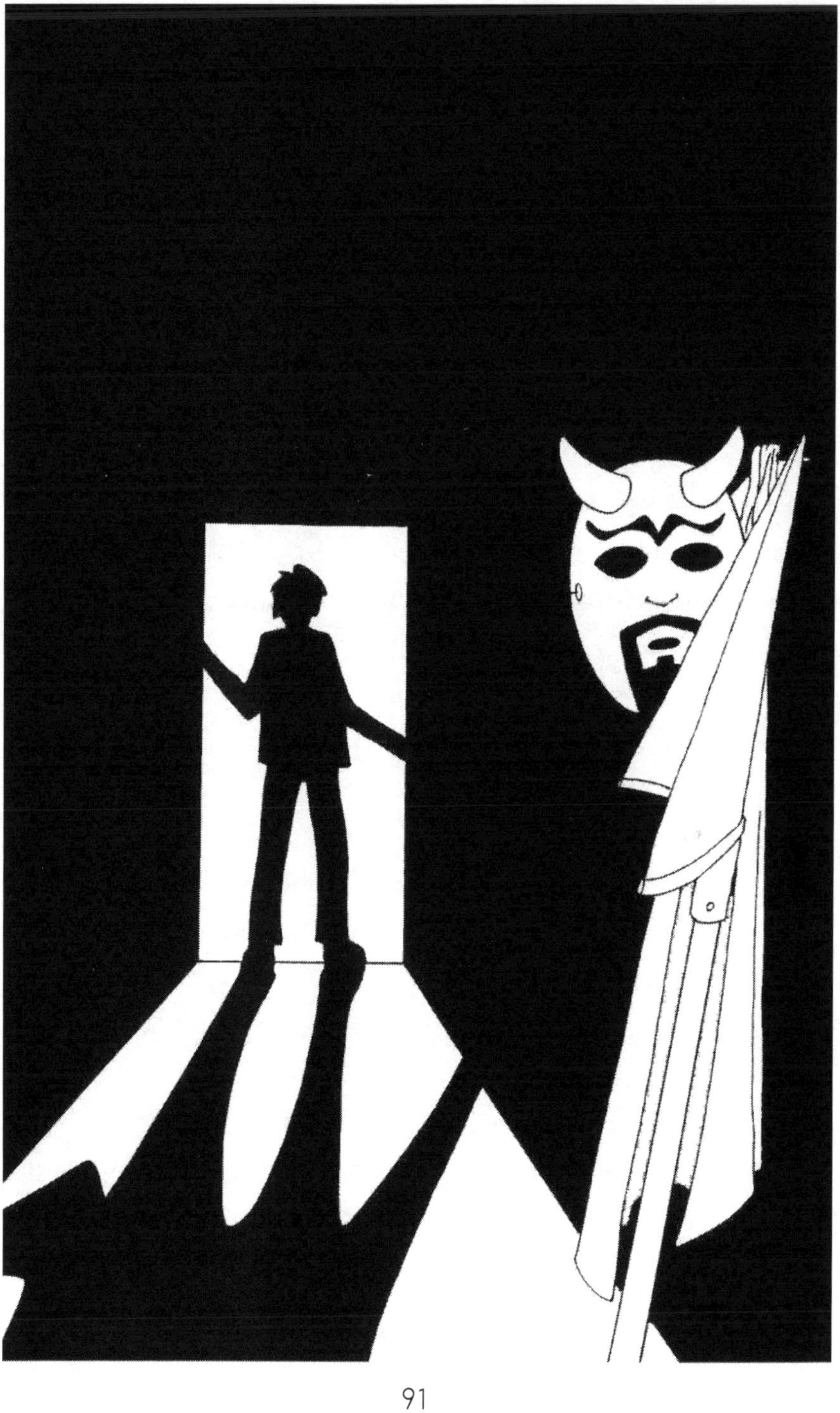

They covered two entire walls, nearly to the ceiling.

"Welcome to your new home, Al."

He placed the skull atop the multitude of others, closed the feeding door on the hatch, and went back outside to fill Albert's grave. By the time he finished, light peeked over the horizon and rose in lines, filtered by the tall pine trees that lined the eastern side of the cemetery. He sat and watched the sun, simultaneously menacing and serene. The morning of Halloween eve had come.

His routine consisted of dry toast to calm the stomach, a cup of coffee, and the cleaning of his shotgun. His hands always shook when loading the shells, frightened that he might have to use them. He shot the bastard once, fifteen years ago. It injured the beast but only long enough for him to drag it back to the hatch and lock it away again.

He looked up at the wall of skulls. "Wish me luck tonight."

When night fell, Robin sat waiting on the porch, gun across his lap. He'd be damned if he were going to let anything happen. Children's laughter sounded from the streets. He watched the kids pass by in their multitude of costumes. They were all risks. They were all in danger.

The banging started as a muffled knock from beneath the house. It grew louder and louder until the chains rattled and the giant padlock slammed against the wood. *It's all riled up*, he thought. *Please don't let it get out tonight.*

It hadn't for fourteen years, but it was a fear that never weakened. It always struck him hard, year after year. The truth of what happened could not be forgotten or ignored.

His grip tightened around the gun when three kids made their way up the front path. They all wore masks. One had a hockey mask, the second a werewolf, and the last a skull. He always left the porch light off and never put up decorations to keep kids from coming to his door, but they didn't seem to care.

"Sorry, kids. Don't have any candy left."

They kept walking toward him.

"Did you hear what I said? No candy here."

The maddening racket in the basement continued.

As they got closer, Robin noticed one of them carried a baseball bat. He swung it around in his hand as any kid would, but in the dark, on Halloween eve, the motion appeared threatening.

"Get the hell off my property!" Robin stood up, but left the gun on his chair.

"Fuck you, old man," the kid with the baseball bat said.

Robin stepped down to confront the teenagers when the one with the bat swung a home run on his knee. It landed with a hard crack and sent him to the ground

"What's all that noise in your house?"

Robin couldn't respond through the screams of his shattered knee.

"Come on, let's go inside and see what he's got."

"Probably nothing good. An old VCR maybe."

"Who cares? Let's just see. If he doesn't have anything, we can just wreck up the place."

"Wait," the werewolf said. "What's this around his neck?" The boy grabbed the chain necklace, on which hung a key.

"A key! He must have a safe or something. Take it."

The boy ripped the chain from his neck without mercy, and tiny silver links scattered in the yard.

"No," Robin grumbled. "Leave it alone."

"Shut up!" The boy wearing a skull mask kicked Robin in the chest.

They left Robin in the grass, his hands wrapped around his injury. He struggled against the pain, gritted his teeth, and tried to stand, but faltered and ended up on his back. Glass shattered in the house, accompanied by what he could only assume was furniture being knocked around. The kids made as much noise as the thing in the basement.

Robin crawled to the porch and grabbed his shotgun. He used it like a cane to hold himself up and painfully made his way inside. He hobbled past the destruction and came to find the cellar door open, silence rising from the staircase. Distinct and unmistakable, the lock clicked open, and the chains slid away from the hatch.

He hobbled down the stairs on one foot as fast as he could. He had to get there in time. He had to stop it.

When he reached the bottom, only one of the boys was still intact. He had his back against the wall of skulls, feet in a pool of blood. The hockey mask shook as his body trembled. A dark patch formed on his jeans and travelled halfway down his leg. He dropped the baseball bat and removed his mask. His eyes widened and bulged from their sockets, the inky black of the pupils blanketing over the surrounding white. Robin knew that look. He'd seen it once before.

He tried to raise the gun but lost his balance and fell back onto the steps. The shotgun came free of his grip and slid down, landing between the kid and the creature. He crawled down and reached for it but stopped, only inches away.

Hot, moldy breath worked its way around his neck and wafted into his nostrils, filling them with the horrible stench that always came from the hatch. The cellar always smelled that way, but its close proximity was like having his face shoved in shit.

Instinct told him to look the other way, to get back upstairs and far away from there. But fear often breaks down that system rather than driving it. Its power to incapacitate held Robin in place, canceling out any other action.

He waited for his guts to be spilled onto the floor in a cascade of carnage. He wondered if it would be like the movies, if he would try scooping them back into his abdomen in a vain attempt at survival. The thought was joined by the immense, excruciating pain that would surely accompany his demise.

The creature's coarse, brown hand reached past Robin and opened its claws as it advanced on the boy. Like curved razors, the multitude of bony fingers sliced at the boy's flesh until the bone had been scraped clean. The claws then flexed like a pair of scissors, and Robin watched in horror as the boy's head rolled across the floor.

The hatch's resident monster lumbered over and picked up the head carefully. It shoved the skull into Robin's chest and forced him to take it.

As the beast crept back toward the hatch, it turned and stared at Robin with vacant black eyes. Its jaw curled into a smile. Then it turned and went down the hatch willingly. It even remained quiet while Robin locked the chains.

He set the three new additions on the wall of skulls and realized he didn't know any of their names. Maybe the news reports that were sure to follow would tell him who the boys were. He'd watch them intently as he'd done once before. Otherwise, they'd sit atop the mass grave in the basement, forever strangers to him.

Outside, as the whispers of Halloween faded away for another year, Robin opened the shed, sighed, and hung the three masks on the wall next to the devil costume.

ON A NIGHT LIKE DEVIL'S NIGHT
BY DANIEL WEAVER

Seven years ago, on Devil's Night, a house burnt down on 17th Street. The arsonist was captured easily enough, and he claimed he'd only intended for the bushes in the front yard to burn, not the whole house. He certainly hadn't meant to kill three people. The police told the press the family had died peacefully in their sleep, but in actuality, as the mischief raged outside, they had all left their beds and were found huddled together in the hallway upstairs, apparently resigning themselves to their fiery deaths that night. Despite protests from many in the town, the flame-addled house was never demolished nor restored, and over the years, it had become a local test of courage for young teens to enter the remains on the anniversary of the family's death.

~

Chris Sanders locked the gate to his family's backyard and walked down Locust Street to where it intersected with 17th Street. The air was thick with clouds of either fog or smoke, but Chris couldn't tell which. It smelled like gunpowder, but with the streamers of blue and green ash raining down from the illegal fireworks that night, everything smelled like gunpowder. Regardless of the source, the clouds hung in the streets, wrapping themselves around everything and muting the small bits of light let out by streetlights and the windows of the few shops that were open, making everything seem much darker than it truly was. It was only 8:30, but it seemed closer to midnight. Men in costumes raced past, leaving destruction and mayhem in their wake, but such things weren't unusual on a night like Devil's Night.

At the intersection, Chris met his two best friends, Derrick Rheinard and Brady O'Malley.

Brady shook his head. "I have a bad feeling about this."

"Come on, you big baby," Rheinard said. "This is our last Devil's Night before you leave for college. Besides, what's the worst that could happen?"

"Well, we could be charged with criminal trespassing," Brady said, "and I know you don't have a future, but I don't particularly want my acceptance to MIT getting turned into a rejection because of your dumb ass."

Chris sighed at their bickering. Brady had always hated Rheinard, and Rheinard had always hated Brady, all the way back to the first grade when the three boys had met. Chris had managed to float in between the two, playing on the football team with Derrick, something Brady would never have considered, and even joining Brady's Dungeons and Dragons campaign during their sophomore year in high school, something Rheinard had said was lame, but Chris didn't mind. He had his friends, and they had their merits to him, otherwise he wouldn't have kept them around. But sometimes, the squabbling got to him.

Chris started to get between them when suddenly, the smooth melody of a bow pulling across a violin string carried a delicate tune down Locust Street. In the midst of the crashing fireworks and general noisiness of Devil's Night, the sound of a violin was out of place—and alarming. The three boys followed the music without realizing they were doing it, and soon saw it was being played by a man standing on a street corner. More alarming than the strangeness of the music was the way the man was dressed. His pants were frayed purple denim, he wore an off white button-down shirt with a tweed jacket over it, and a look of forlorn sadness permanently etched the rubber mask which hung upon his face.

"Nice outfit," Rheinard said, raising a hand to pound fists with the clown, who he assumed to be another teenager.

But the man did not raise a hand to meet Rheinard's. Instead, he put his violin and bow to his side, locking his plastic gaze with the three boys.

"Yeah, screw you then," Rheinard said as he and Chris walked past the man without another glance.

But Brady couldn't take his eyes away from the clown. Seeing people dressed in strange costumes was not unusual on a night like Devil's Night—in fact, the boys had already crossed paths with Michael Myers, Freddy Krueger, and

Ghostface without as much as a second glance. But the clown unsettled Brady so much that eventually, he was turned entirely around, walking backwards down the street, afraid to look away from the man.

"Baby boy afraid of the spooky pranks?" Rheinard struck his fist into Brady's arm, causing him to instinctively turn and nearly swing at his not-so-friend.

"There's just something about..." Brady turned back to the clown but found nothing on the street corner in its place.

"Come on, guys, let's keep going," Chris said, and they all started walking again.

"All I'm saying," Rheinard started, resuming a conversation that Brady hadn't heard the start of, "is that a year off before college isn't going to kill you. A few more weekend parties, a few more half-assed ideas—"

"I'm going to be home from Pitt every weekend," Chris said, chuckling softly.

"Guys," Brady whispered, and both boys turned to face him. "I really don't think this is a good idea."

"Quit being such a baby," Rheinard said. "We're already halfway there."

"Yeah, so, halfway is good enough," Brady said. "Let's just head back, okay?"

"Or here's a better option," said Rheinard. "You put on your big boy pants, and you shut the hell up, okay?"

"Rheinard," Chris said quietly, warning his friend to cool it.

Rheinard pushed Chris away. "No, it's been ten years of

this, and I'm tired of it," he said. "This is our last Devil's Night together, and I'm not going to let Brady ruin it."

"Well, I'm not going to let some idiot ruin my scholarship to MIT," Brady snapped back. "We all know you'll be stuck here for the rest of your life, but some of us want to get out."

At that, Rheinard lunged forward, and despite Chris's best attempts to hold him back, Rheinard managed to deliver a stiff punch to Brady's jaw. It was the first and the last real punch of the smaller boy's life. Brady fell to the ground, and Chris managed to wrap both arms around Rheinard this time, stopping him from mounting the smaller boy and rearranging his face.

Fireworks crashed overhead as Rheinard stood above the cowering Brady, his fist raised high for a punch he'd never throw. Suddenly, there was a flash of blue and red lights, and the night was interrupted by the familiar wails of a police siren.

"What in the hell is going on here, boys?" A police officer stepped out of his vehicle as Brady scampered to his feet.

"Nothing, Officer." Chris released his grip on Rheinard after the two shared a look that said 'be on your best behavior.'

"Yeah, Officer, nothing." Rheinard straightened his jacket as he spoke. "My friend here just tripped, and I was helping him up."

"That so?" the officer asked, looking at Brady, a fresh tendril of blood pouring from his nose.

"Yeah," Brady said, wiping his wrist against his broken nose. "I tripped."

"Be honest," the officer said. "You boys causing trouble? Because we've been getting some unusual calls from this part of town tonight."

"No, sir," Chris said quickly, but he wondered what sorts of things would be considered unusual on a night like Devil's Night. "We're just out for a little walk."

"If I have to come after you three tonight, there'll be hell to pay," the officer said. "Take that as a warning."

The cop returned to his car and drove away, leaving the three alone again.

"Fuck you, Rheinard," Brady said, walking into the darkened street. "I hope you die in this town, do you understand me?"

Chris called after him, but Brady simply raised a hand with a middle finger and disappeared into the darkness. In the distance, Chris heard what he thought might have been a cackle of laughter, or maybe it was a bow madly sawing away at some high note on a violin. It was unnerving, and it made his stomach turn, but again, these things weren't unusual on a night like Devil's Night.

Chris shook his head. "You know, you're kind of an asshole, Rheinard."

"Hey!" Rheinard punched Chris on the arm softly, much softer than he had punched Brady. He had always hated Brady and had been waiting years for the chance to get him with a good right hook. Chris though? He didn't hate him, not at all. In fact, though he would never say it, Derrick Rheinard loved Chris Sanders. He was like the brother he never had, and to be honest, he hated the thought of losing him.

"What's wrong?" Chris asked him after a moment of silence.

"Nothing, just thinking about the future," Rheinard answered after a pause, and it was the truth. The reason he got so upset at Brady was because he knew the boy's words were true. Rheinard would be stuck here for the rest of his life. He would die here. Chris had his scholarship to Pitt, Brady was going to MIT, and he would be stuck here next fall, working at his dad's garage, and taking classes at the community college.

"Look, there's nothing wrong with staying local for a few years before heading off to university," Chris said. "Hell, it's probably the better idea. It'll save you a ton of money."

"I don't give a damn about the money, Chris."

"Then what is it?"

"Just forget about it, okay?" Rheinard said.

The two walked in silence again for a few moments.

"I got it," Chris said, snapping his fingers together. "It's Roni, isn't it?"

Roni, or Veronica as her parents called her, had been Rheinard's girlfriend for the last seven months, and Chris knew that she had already received an acceptance letter to a university in Vermont, leaving her a dozen hours away from 'her love.'

"Shit, no," Rheinard said, laughing softly. "I just hate the idea of you going away to Pitt, and me staying back here alone, okay?" Rheinard's eyes were locked on the ground beneath him. "I know it's stupid, but I've known you for longer than I haven't, and I don't want to go through making a new best friend."

"That's not stupid," Chris said. "I completely get it. But you can't ask me to stay behind because you'll be uncomfortable."

"And I never would ask you that," Rheinard said seriously, kicking stones with his feet. "But I'm allowed to be upset about it, aren't I?"

Chris stopped walking, and when Rheinard realized he had, he turned to face him.

"What's wrong?" Rheinard asked.

Chris stepped forward and pulled his friend into a tight hug.

"Chris, what the-"

"Shut up," Chris said, and Rheinard did. "Just shut the hell up, okay? You're my best friend, and I love you, you got that?"

Rheinard said nothing, choosing to simply accept the hug and soon he returned it, despite knowing what people might think about them for doing so. After a moment, the two moved apart and said nothing else on the topic, instead continuing on towards the burned down house. Illegal fireworks crashed in the sky above them as younger kids ran by with rolls of toilet paper in their backpacks, knowing they would never be punished for what they did. And still, these things weren't unusual on a night like Devil's Night.

This placid feeling between Chris and Rheinard lasted several minutes as they approached the center of town, where a majority of the normally open businesses were closed tonight, and the crowds were gathered in force. Through the mess of people, Chris spotted a familiar tweed jacket moving at the back of the crowd, but as soon as he saw it, it was gone. He assumed his mind was playing tricks on him, but no, he saw it again out of the corner of his eye. It wasn't the tweed jacket this time, but a flash of ripped purple pants, again moving through the outskirts of the crowd. It was the clown, the clown from the street corner that had scared Brady only a few minutes earlier. He knew he was being paranoid, but he couldn't help think that this clown was following him. It made no sense to think that, but something told him he was right.

"Hey, Rheinard, what's the deal with that clown?" He pointed at the spot where he'd last seen the man move, but again, he was gone.

"What clown?" Rheinard asked him, looking where his friend had pointed. Chris began to tell him 'never mind' when suddenly a large festival of balloons in shades of reds and yellows and blues and greens, which seemed almost luminescent in the fog or smoke-filled street, rose into the air on the other side of the crowd. Chris watched the dozens or even hundreds of balloons ascend into the darkness, and he was almost sure he was losing his mind until he saw the other members of the crowd turn and gasp as they looked upon the multitude rising and disappearing into the blackened sky. While many things could pass for ordinary, this show was unusual even on a night like Devil's Night.

"What in the hell..." Chris heard Rheinard start saying, in wonder of the spectacle that arose before him, but all Chris could focus on was the shrill cackle of laughter he heard, a cackle that almost sounded like some mad scratching on tightened strings. His skin crawled again, and his stomach turned once more as he recognized the sound.

Once the balloons vanished, Chris and Rheinard left the square and were again alone on the quiet, small town street. The fog or smoke had mostly lifted on this side of town, and the two boys could see the few blocks ahead to where the charred remains of that old house stood. In a way, that was comforting to Chris. When the trio had met just a half hour before, Chris's confidence had been high that no problems would come to them during their travels. However, with Brady leaving and the strange things they kept seeing, Chris was more than a little flustered. Seeing the house was like the sight of dry land after a lengthy sea voyage.

A yellow Chevy Cavalier, the bright color like a beacon on the darkened street, drove past them to a stop sign, switched to reverse, and then parked next to them. A rear window lowered, and both boys were surprised to see Rheinard's girlfriend Roni sitting in the backseat.

"Hey, babe!" she shouted to Rheinard.

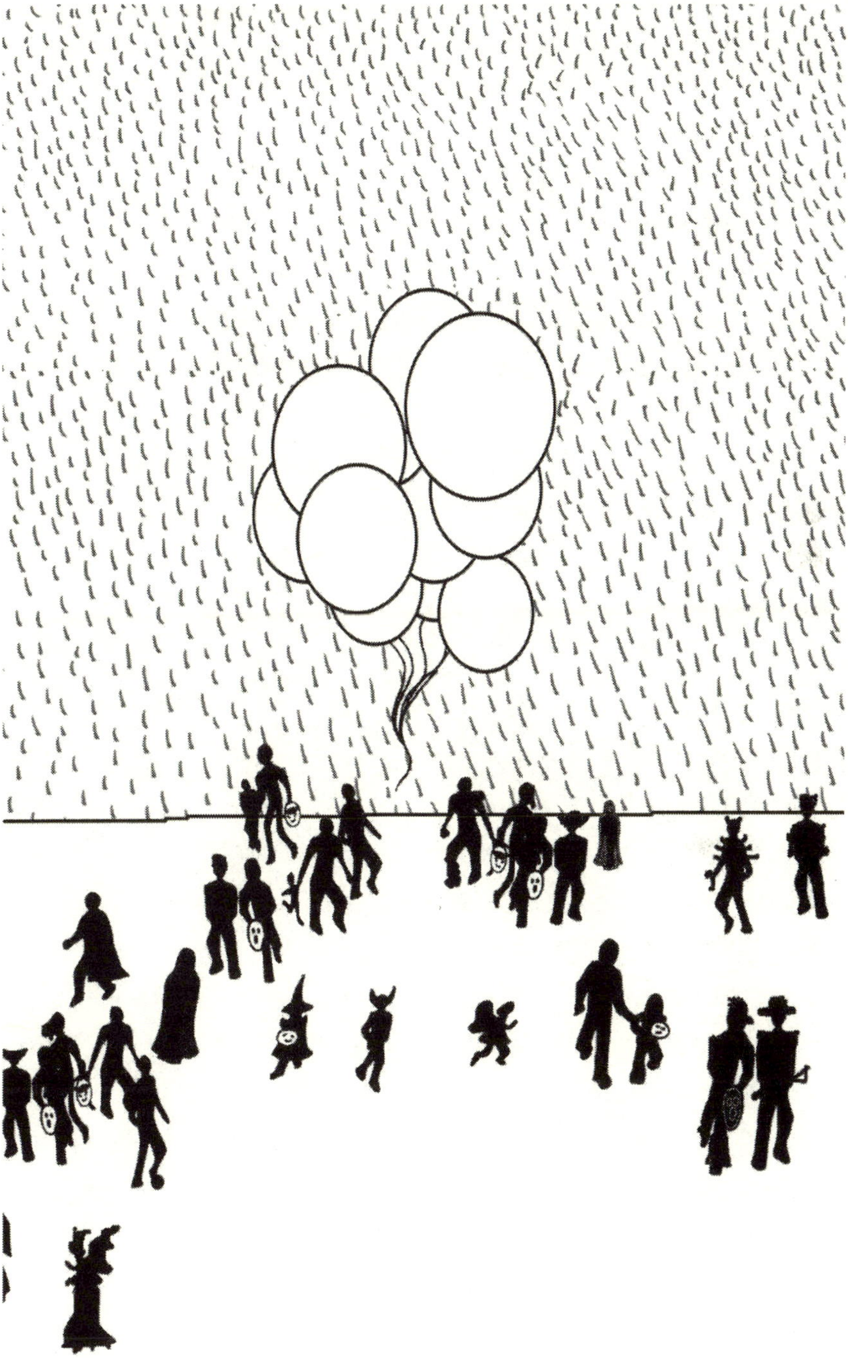

"Hey, what are you doing?" he asked, surprised to see her.

"We," she started, gesturing at herself and her brother who was driving the car, "are going to a concert. Do you guys want to come?"

Rheinard turned to Chris, but Chris shook his head.

"You go," he said. "I want to see to the house."

Rheinard smiled. "Thank you," he said. "For everything. Even the... you know."

Chris laughed as his friend got in the car and drove away through the suburban streets.

Suddenly, Chris Sanders was entirely alone on Devil's Night.

~

The house was smaller than Chris remembered it being, but he assumed the fire could be blamed for that. As a child, he'd thought of this house as a mansion, with its finely shingled roof, perfect paint job of reds, browns, and beiges, and its meticulously manicured lawn. Now, seven years after the fire, the house was a trap of charred walls, broken windows, and overgrown grass that hid who knows what beneath them. Standing on the sidewalk in front of the house, his hands resting on the metal gate that separated the inside from the outside of the property, black paint still flecking off its surface after years of neglect, Chris Sanders was afraid.

After a moment staring into the remains of the once grand house, the hair on Chris's arms and neck began to stand on edge, and he got the unshakeable feeling that he was being watched. At first, he assumed there must be other Devil's Night revelers hiding in the abandoned house, their eyes set on him to decide if it was safe to continue their vandalism. But after looking through each broken window, he saw no other mischief makers. Deciding instead that he was psyching himself out, he placed his hand on the gate's lock and started to pull it open.

"You sure you want to do that?" said a gravelly, smoke-filled voice from behind him.

Frightened, Chris looked behind him, and standing only inches away was a man wearing a clown's mask, ripped purple denim pants and a tweed jacket. He stank of gunpowder, and from this distance, Chris could clearly hear the man's heavy breath as it left his nose and struck the thick plastic in front of it.

"You're him... you're... the clown," Chris stammered.

The man cocked his head inquisitively. "Oh, no, no," he said. "I am so much more than that."

"Have you been following me?"

"I follow all," the man said, his words muted by the plastic mask. "And all eventually find me."

"I saw you at the street corner on Locust," Chris said. "And again at the square. What do you want with me?"

"Tonight, it was not you I came for," the clown rasped.

"Then what is it?"

"Your two friends."

"Well, they're gone now, and it's just me, okay?" Chris

said.

"I know," the clown replied, simply, and it almost seemed like there was joy in his permanent grimace.

"Know what?"

"They're gone."

Chris shuddered. "What do you want with me?"

"To see what you do next," the clown said. "There are two options: enter or walk away. One ends in life, the other in death."

"What are you talking about? Who are you?" Chris asked.

"I am Death itself," the clown said.

Chris laughed in the clown's face. "That's a good one, man," he said, reaching out and putting a hand on his shoulder, "but if you'll excuse me, I have..."

"Brady O'Malley would have been dead in twelve months," the clown said, interrupting Chris swiftly, "driven mad by the pressures of MIT. Instead, I had to take him tonight for venturing out on Devil's Night."

"I need to go home," Chris tried to say, but the words wouldn't come, and part of him feared the clown had taken his power of speech. He tried to walk away, but the clown reached a hand out and pushed him back into the metal gate behind him. Even after the hand was gone, Chris still couldn't move away.

"Derrick Rheinard would have lived another seventeen years," the clown continued, "but would spend the last eleven of them in prison after a domestic disturbance left his wife of seven months dead. Instead, I took him tonight, with his girlfriend and her brother. These things aren't unusual on a night like Devil's Night."

"This isn't funny," Chris managed to say, though his throat was dry and the words were raspy.

"This isn't a joke," the man said. "I took their lives early, because they strayed from their path."

"Are you going to kill me?" Chris struggled to ask.

"Oh no." The clown shook his head. "You have so much more to live for."

"I can't move," Chris said.

"I can't trust you not to go into the house."

"I won't," he answered. "I swear I won't."

Before the words were even out of his mouth, the force that was pinning him to the gate had lifted, and his body moved for what felt like the first time. Looking up, the clown was gone, and Chris wasn't sure if he'd ever been there at all.

Suddenly, a police car rolled through the fog and smoke, stopping in front of where Chris stood.

"Hey, kid, what are you doing?" the officer barked at Chris.

"I'm just walking home," Chris said, shrugging as he spoke in a voice that was not quite his.

The cop nodded toward the burnt down house. "You trying to go in there?"

"No, sir," Chris said.

"You put that there?" the cop asked, pointing.

Chris turned to see a dozen balloons in reds and blues and oranges and yellows tied to the black metal gate behind him.

"No, sir," he said.

"Goddamn kids," the cop said. "Listen, you need a ride home?"

"I think I'll be okay," Chris said.

"Be safe out there, kid," the cop said. "We had a lot of crazy shit tonight. One kid got stabbed to death about a half hour ago, and I just got a call about a pretty bad wreck outside town. Kids probably couldn't see through this goddamn smoke."

Chris said nothing, and after a moment, the police officer pulled away, leaving Chris alone again in the darkened street. Over the sound of the engine rumbling, and the wheels rolling along the street, Chris was almost certain he could hear a cackle of laughter, and it made his stomach turn, but again, that wasn't unusual on a night like Devil's Night.

THE SEPTEMBER CEREMONY
BY GWENDOLYN KISTE

The last day in September was an auspicious one for the family. Fall was upon us, and with it came the seasonal preparations of the estate.

First and foremost, cobwebs were draped from the chandelier, and live spiders accompanied the decor. As usual, the creeping creatures spun the most luxurious white lace wherever we missed a spot.

Scissors shredded any sections of the curtains that weren't already ragged, and one by one, my pale progeny removed hinges and handles and other accoutrements from the bureaus and dressers in all the bedrooms.

When we were done, the house was a decrepit mess—and far more superb for it.

Like every year before and every year for as long as the family endures, the abiding sense of macabre merriment sent our skeletons—both the ones beneath our skin and the ones beneath our floorboards—all aflutter.

"If only my bones could already be in the crypt," Carolyn, the youngest, said as she tossed shriveled leaves onto the vintage rug in the parlor. "Then I wouldn't have to do so much work."

Smiling, I served her a more than generous portion of blackbird pie and beckoned all three of my daughters to the table. "Death will happen soon enough, darling."

"No, it won't," she said and huffed. "If I'm particularly unlucky, I could live in this meat package another eighty years."

"Be grateful we can carry on the family traditions." Anjelica plopped into a seat, and a lovely cloud of dust puffed from the upholstery like a spritz of perfume. "If it weren't for us, this whole property could be torn down and replaced with some tacky retail plaza."

The oldest at sweet sixteen—sweet as cyanide, of course—Bebe shooed a plague of rats from her chair. "Mother? If this place is razed after our deaths, can we haunt the shoppers and shopkeepers?"

"Yes, love," I said. "But let's just hope it doesn't come to that. I'd hate to think of the chandelier being replaced with fluorescent lighting."

Carolyn shuddered. "A Black Friday indeed!"

My beautiful daughters—their long hair as dark as their glorious little souls—tittered and conspired over dessert.

Yes, the end of September had indeed arrived.

We finished the plates of pie, and after picking feathers from between our teeth, we set about the final preparations. Bebe took the cloaks, and I gathered enough candles to illuminate any cemetery in the world. Fortunately, we only had to light one: our own family's cemetery, which was packed to the topsoil with shrouds and sepulchers.

"Does everyone have their slips of paper for the ceremony?" I asked, and the girls nodded jovially before we departed for the backyard mausoleums.

Anjelica skipped across the dead grass, the sun vanishing between the trees like a bashful spirit. "I can't wait to see Grandma!"

"I don't want to see her at all," Carolyn said with a scowl. "She's had almost a full year to visit, and she hasn't attempted to haunt us. Not even once."

"Perhaps she thought it too vulgar," I said. "Your grandmother always was the primmest of the family."

"Too prim to visit her grandchildren?" Carolyn shook her head. "I don't care if I never see the old lady again!"

At that, an eldritch mist floated through the cracks of the sagging pillars and proceeded to pursue Carolyn around the yard. The nine-year-old giggled like it was a most splendid game and raced from one end of the graveyard to the other.

"You can't catch me, Grandma!" She shrieked and galloped in circles around Anjelica, who just rolled her eyes and kicked a headstone.

"Who dare disturb me?" a voice demanded from the ground, and the two younger girls howled, eager to outrun both a ghostly fog as well as a curmudgeon of a ghoul.

"When's father arriving?" Bebe studied me, her light eyes a perfect match to his.

"Soon," I said, though she knew I was lying.

Even though the ceremony was a sacred occasion, my husband was a terrible bother when it came to dates and times. Door-to-door sales isn't as easy as it used to be, particularly in the bloodletting racket. So many regulations these days! And so difficult to smuggle his sanguine goods past customs.

"Are we ready yet?" Carolyn scurried past me, the mist still in fast pursuit. "Grandma keeps getting in my hair!"

Anjelica stomped her foot. "I don't want to start without Dad!"

"Well, we can't wait any longer." Bebe tossed her sisters their brown cloaks.

"I'm not wearing mine," Carolyn said just because she could.

I sighed. "That's fine. It's more symbolic than anything."

"You should respect tradition," Anjelica whispered, and the mist swirled in agreement. "You don't want bad luck, do you?"

Carolyn grumbled and pulled the dark velvet around her face. The cloak was too big, but like her siblings before her, she would grow into it.

I set my burlap bag of supplies on the nearest burial vault and donned my own garb, which was royal blue to separate me as leader of the group.

"I wish mine was that color too," Carolyn muttered, and her sisters hushed her.

I lit a row of candles. "Have each of you practiced your parts of the invocation?"

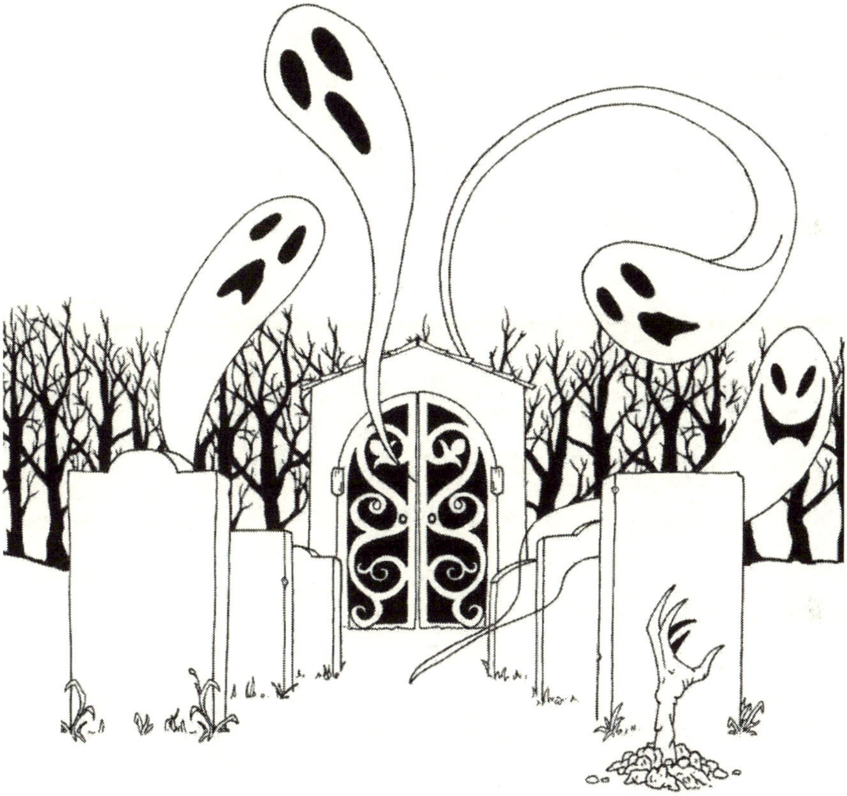

They nodded. A wolf on some distant hill cried in refrain, and it wasn't even a full moon.

Bebe rolled her eyes. "I can't believe we're incorporating modern technology into the chant this year."

"We need to stay timely," I said. "Otherwise, we become anachronisms, and the whole thing falls apart."

"I guess," Bebe said, twirling a strand of glossy hair around her thin fingers. "It just seems so... crass."

"Any other objections?"

Besides the ghoul still complaining about Anjelica "vandalizing" his headstone, everyone was quiet.

"Then let us begin."

Our fingers dug into the ground, and we each brought a handful of earth to our chest.

"Ancestors," I said. "Hear us now."

We tossed the soil into the air, and one after another, the visages of phantoms and demons materialized and leered at us through the moonlight.

"Hello, Uncle Ray," I said to one.

"Greetings, Aunt Emily," Bebe said to another.

"I'm not talking to you, Grandmother," Carolyn said, her lips twitching as she tried to subdue a smile.

I waved to my mother as her delicate features became solid once more.

"October is almost here again," I said. "We set you free from this place for thirty-one days. We set you free to wreak Halloween havoc in the name of our family!"

An ethereal green shot out of every crevice in the ground

and the granite. Even after partaking in forty-five ceremonies, the moment still took my breath away.

"Let Trick or Treat be equal parts of both." The slip of paper between her fingers, Anjelica pronounced each word with the melodramatic flair of a hammy Shakespearean actor. "Use your alchemy to transform milk chocolate into caustic cherry bubblegum."

A faction of imps rotated overhead, the eerie voices intimating a calliope of out-of-tune dirges.

"And while taunting children with toothbrushes and floss in their Halloween satchels, do not let the adults escape your wrath," I said, picking up the lines reserved for my husband. "Create campy, lewd costumes that in retrospect will embarrass those foolish adults who wear them."

Cackles spilled into the night as if the creatures were escaping us, as if we couldn't contain them. But we continued. We always continued.

"During festive gatherings, whisper into their ears," Bebe said like a witch hunched over a cauldron. "Tempt them with ambrosia and convince them to take horrible selfies they will then post to every form of social media."

The cacophony hit its fever pitch. Our kin twirled and pirouetted over us, and a kaleidoscope of fog spread along the horizon like an Aurora Borealis of the dead.

Carolyn stared at her strip of paper. "Mother, I don't know what this means."

The dancing demons ceased their revelry, and we all gaped at the pintsize killjoy.

"I thought you said you practiced."

"Well, I did," she said, her feet fidgeting and stepping on the edges of her oversized cloak. "But I can't say it like the rest of you. I don't know where the emphasis goes."

"Give us a moment," I said to the spirits as I kneeled next to my daughter.

"What's this word?" She pointed at 'autumnal', and I pronounced it for her.

"And try stressing 'decree', 'grace', and 'free', okay?"

She nodded and inhaled. "With this summons, we... we do *decree*. Enjoy the autum... autumnal *grace* and for this... month, be *free*! "

The spell complete, the specters catapulted in every direction, wailing with glee as they glided through the sky. It took a full five minutes for the crypts to empty, and the entire time, the power from the mass exodus was so strong that my daughters and I levitated from the rich earth.

My mother bid farewell to me and her grandchildren before soaring off with the Gilded Age branch of the family, fringe dresses and long-stemmed cigarettes in tow.

Always last, the cantankerous ghoul climbed from his vault, shaking an antique cane as he went.

With all the spirits departed, the four of us mortals drifted back to the ground, our feet buried in the soil as if we had never left.

Anjelica squealed. "That was the best ceremony ever! Ever! Ever!"

"It should certainly grant us good luck for the next year,"

I said and collected the candles that had by now retreated to wicks.

"Did you see them?" Carolyn jumped up and down. "It was like the best fireworks in the world!"

"I'm glad Grandmother's going with them," Bebe said. "About time she had some fun."

Hands grasped in a circle, the girls danced about the graveyard and sang one of the more upbeat elegies they had learned from the ancestors long ago.

Like every year, things felt empty afterwards. The murmurs that haunted the grounds the other eleven months had departed, and though profoundly lonely, I smiled, certain the Halloween antics would be extra morbid this year.

"Did I miss all the fun?" a voice asked from the rickety gate.

"Daddy!"

The girls scampered to their father and almost knocked over his hopelessly lanky form in the process.

"You did miss it, Dad," Carolyn said. "Even Grandmother was here."

"Oh, I'm not so sure I'm sad about missing her," he said and glanced at me. "She never was my biggest fan."

"She warmed up to you." I strolled toward him and clasped my ice-cold fingers around his. "Warmed up the best any of us can."

With whispered secrets that weren't really secrets at all, the grinning girls returned to their interpretive Halloween dance.

"I'm sorry, love," he said to me. "A family in Romania made a last-minute order. Blood in bulk, enough to fill a warehouse. The paperwork took forever."

"Don't worry," I said as distant church bells struck twelve. "The girls were magnificent."

Hand in hand, I led him to the center of the cemetery where we joined our daughters, crooning and frolicking late into the evening.

After all, October was now upon us. And it was going to be a beauty.

HALL 'O WEEN PARTIE!
BY TROY BLACKFORD

"What is it really?" Marshall McDonigal asked, his face scrunched up not out of disgust, but mistrust.

"I told you," Margaret Huntington said, trying to keep the mood light, but ominous. She blinked some of the green witch's makeup out of her eyes. "It's *braaaaains*."

"That's incredibly unlikely," Marshall said.

Margaret's shoulders slumped a little, but she perked back up as a new thought occurred to her.

"It's *terribly* unlikely, Marshall." She cackled in a way she hoped sounded rather witchly. "But it's the truth: it's the brains of a little boy who said the exact same thing at our *last* Halloween party!"

Marshall didn't even bother to keep his face scrunched.

"If that were the case, why haven't they fully decomposed by now?"

Margaret sighed and didn't even try to conceal it.

"Alright, you caught me. It's spaghetti. Thanks for playing along."

Marshall smiled at this. Margaret hoped, for a second,

that he was deciding to lighten up.

"I'm glad, Mrs. H. Because if it really *were* brains, I'd have to report you to the authorities, and I really don't want to do that."

"Run along, Marshall," said Margaret, her internal organs cooling at a shocking rate. "And don't ruin it for any of the other kids."

But Marshall was already backing away. He was heading back to the endless two-liters of soda, and the bowls of candy and popcorn, and the 'all you could watch' Netflix buffet, streaming endless tales of ghoulies and ghosties and things that go bump in the night.

"Ruin *what*, Mrs. H?" asked Marshall, draining the last droplets of Grape Crush from his black and orange party cup.

Margaret didn't even try to answer; she just waved him on.

Ahh, well, she thought. *What could you expect from a kid who shows up to a Halloween party dressed as a bank teller?* She was honestly kind of surprised he didn't come dressed as a 'Systems Analyst' or a 'Support Services Coordinator.' Surely the other kids weren't going to be like this when their turns came?

"Why are you cooking that?" her daughter, Felicia, had asked an hour before. "Nobody is going to want to eat spaghetti at a Halloween party."

Margaret had assured her that she had a plan, and that her little friends would be delighted. She could remember her first Halloween party, almost as clearly as she could remember (slightly) more recent events like her wedding, and Felicia's birth, and grabbing a handful of squishy 'brains' had been one of the horrifying highlights. But none of Felicia's friends were biting. The grape eyeballs weren't doing the trick, either.

"That's morbid," said Amanda, who was a fair degree less stodgy than Marshall—she, at least, was dressed as a licensed character that Margaret didn't recognize rather than a job fair reject.

"It's supposed to be a *Halloween* party," Margaret said.

"Halloween *party*, not Halloween *barf fest*, Mrs. H."

When did they all start calling her that? Margaret didn't want to be called Missus any more than she wanted her name to be 'H.' Amanda trotted back out to the Netflix-binge. Margaret thought it was incongruous: these kids got a bigger dose of fantasy than any prior generation, but they had surprisingly inflexible imaginations.

Margaret was just about to put her covered bowls of spaghetti and grapes away, thinking that every kid on the guest list had already come through, when a bright white streak of movement caught her peripheral vision. She looked up and almost laughed aloud at what she saw. A kid about a head shorter than all the other second and third graders toddled in, wearing the oldest Halloween costume there was: a white sheet, with holes cut out for the eyes. In the dim, flickering light of the LED candles Margaret had set up in the kitchen (for *ambiance*, she had explained to Felicia, who had rolled her eyes), Margaret couldn't make out his face through the small, circular cutouts. But whoever he was, at least this kid knew what Halloween was *for*.

He waddled up to the first of the bowls and tilted his head back to look up at her. The impression Margaret got was of a baleful puppy. She couldn't help but smile.

"Feel what I have in my bowl, *if you dare*, little ghost!"

He obediently reached out two arms, poking out two sheet-proboscises. His costume extended almost to his shoes, and he seemed too fully committed to his role to pull the sheet up and over his hands. Margaret turned the laughter bubbling up inside her into a quick, half-chortling witch's cackle. She didn't want the little guy to realize she was laughing at him, after all.

"It's *brains*, young ghosty!" she said, after she had given his hands sufficient time to palpate the grotesquery.

Again, the little head tilted back, and the perfectly round holes in the sheet made the child's unseen eyes look almost preternaturally large with wonder. The hand-fronds shot out of the bowl and back down by his sides.

"Do you want to feel what I have in *this* bowl?" Margaret asked, getting into her role as black-hearted sorceress. Even though her green face paint was running rather noticeably in some patches by now, she felt more like a witch than ever. "It's even more gruesome!"

The kid shook his head, but in that highly vigorous manner that indicates pleasure at being asked, rather than meaning *no*.

"Ahh, but what ghost would pass up such a rare opportunity?"

The figure seemed to consider this before shrugging and stuffing his two blanketed pseudopods into the second bowl. He looked up at her immediately, evidently wanting to hear what he had stuck his hands into before he rubbed it too vigorously. She tried to smile a bewitching smile.

"This, my young ghost, is a bowl full of *eyeballs*."

His two hands were out of the bowl almost as quickly as when she had told him the first was full of brains, but they did not go down to his sides this time. He raised his hands to his face like he was going to cry. For a second, Margaret worried she had upset him. These kids were, after all, only in the second grade.

Before she could decide what was happening, he had slapped his palms to his eyeholes, and Margaret dropped the bowl of grapes to the floor where it shattered. Grapes shot across the floor like a broken rack of billiard balls. The boy had jammed a grape into each of the ragged, black circles in the sheet covering his face. Margaret felt like a fool for dropping the bowl, but the effect was creepy. Creepier than her bowl of spaghetti had ever been, that was for sure.

"Who are you?" she found herself saying and felt even stupider. "Are you Clarice's little brother?"

That would certainly explain a few things.

The head shook back and forth slowly, the two grape eyes leering out with obscene avidity.

"Well, who are you then?" Margaret couldn't believe she

was talking like this to a second grader. Was she really that rattled? Still, she found herself powerless to stop. "Who invited you?"

The cloth deformed, bulging outwards, as a single, accusatory finger pointed Margaret's way.

"Oh, really," she said, bending down to pick up the grapes and the ceramic shards of broken bowl. Any excuse to not have to look at those ridiculous grapes stuck in that face. On *his face*, she told herself. *You mean on his face*. She dumped all of the waste away except for, she noticed, a final piece. "When did I invite you, oh silent one?"

As she picked up the largest of the broken pieces, a folded, orange card hit the floor beneath the ghost's feet with a heavy *slap*, as though he had been a hen and this construction paper creation had been his egg. For a fleeting moment, no sense of recognition touched Margaret. She reached out to pick it up, not registering the child's worn, long-out-of-fashion Converse All-Stars sneakers.

She didn't scream when her mind finally latched onto the distant memory. She didn't scream. She simply looked at the card, which she had made herself almost thirty years before, and blinked.

"*HALL 'O WEEN PARTIE!*" the front screamed in lurid magic marker scrawl. "Where: Margie Bargie's." *How long had it been since she had called herself* 'Margie Bargie?' "When: Thursday, October 16th." It didn't say what year, but Margie Bargie remembered. It had been 1986, and she had attended the party dressed as Christa McAuliffe, the teacher selected by NASA for the opportunity to be burnt alive in the Space Shuttle Challenger disaster.

"Maybe I *am* morbid," she said to herself.

Maybe she'd always been.

She looked at the card, at the crude drawing of a pumpkin she had attempted, outlining it in green when her first-grade self had realized that orange-on-orange wasn't the most visible of color combinations.

"Where did you get this?" she said as she rose, but she was afraid she knew the answer.

The hand shot forward again, pointing right at her.

"Joey?"

The little figure nodded.

Joseph DeBattista. There was a name she hadn't thought of for well over a decade. It hadn't always been like that, though. No, there was a time where she had thought of the doomed little guy all the time. It had taken years of counseling to get over her sense that she had killed him as surely as if she had done it herself.

"I'm sorry," she blurted out. Maybe *get over* was too strong a phrase to describe how she had dealt with it. Maybe not thinking about it all the time really *wasn't* the same as feeling at peace with what had happened. "I'm so sorry, Joseph."

The little figure beneath the blanket merely shrugged. The grape eyes stared out blankly. Silence spun out a moment longer. Margaret spoke.

"I never meant for that to happen. I just wanted you to

come to my party." Giant green drops were landing on her black witch's robe, and she realized she was crying her makeup off. "I am so, *so* sorry."

The ghost shook its head, reached a hand out towards her. She gripped it fiercely, feeling the tears come harder now.

"I never meant... I just thought..."

Joey took his unencumbered hand and raised it to his face in a *'shh'* gesture. He stepped toward her and hugged her around the knees. She didn't know how long she stood there like that, clutching his tiny head—a head that never had a chance to grow beyond age seven, a head that had been crushed by a semi a little over a month after the first episode of Oprah had aired—to her waist and bawling noiselessly.

She didn't know, but it couldn't have been too long.

"Jeez, Mom: are you *crying*?" Felicia asked, standing in the doorway. She flipped the light on. "What's wrong? Someone poke holes in your sheet?"

Margaret looked down at the empty sheet she was clutching and blinked absently.

"You dropped your grapes," Felicia said, trying to be helpful.

"Look at this," Margaret said, holding up her old Halloween party invitation.

"What the heck is that?" Felicia asked, squinting in the fluorescent lights, which seemed shockingly bright to Margaret.

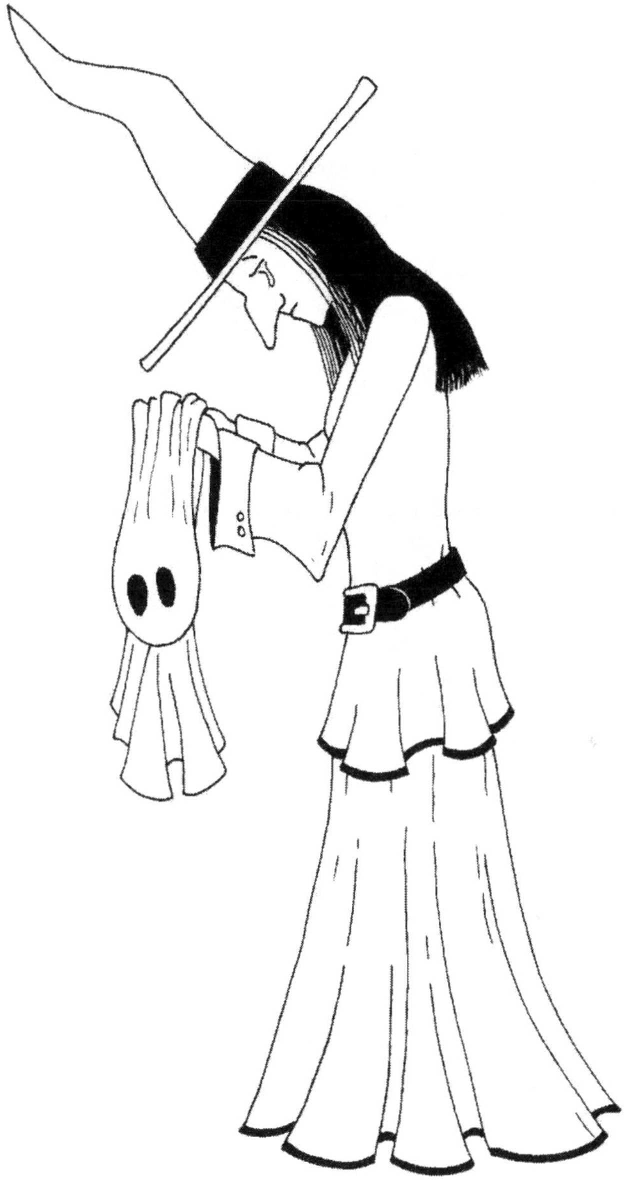

"It's an invitation to a Halloween party my parents threw for me when I was your age."

"And you used *paper*?" Felicia asked.

Yes, thought Margaret, *because I grew up in the Stone Age when kids gave paper invitations to their friends, and* yes *we called them 'invitations' and not 'invites.'* Aloud, she said: "It was easier to write on than aluminum."

She threw the sheet over her shoulder, set the invitation on the counter, along with the remaining shard of ceramic, and headed to the door.

"I need to fix my witch makeup."

"Aren't you going to pick up your grapes?"

She paused, turned around, looked at the two lonely grapes lying there on the floor.

"I don't think so," she said.

Felicia raised an eyebrow.

"Are you okay, Mom?"

Margie Bargie smiled.

"I think so," she said.

"Good," Felicia said, spinning around on one foot and taking two quick hops. "We need you to put in your Netflix password again when you're done with the makeup, because Donny reset the account thingamabobber."

Of course he did. Donny was going to be making computer viruses by the time he was twelve, at the rate he was going. Not very clever ones, either.

"No problem," Margaret said.

Felicia bounded back out into the living room, back out

into the throng of well-costumed little kids, and little Margie Bargie kept smiling out of Margaret Huntington's face, starting to feel like maybe she could finally forgive herself for something that had happened long ago, during a party a lot like this one, a party where everybody kept wondering why little Joey DeBattista was running so late—hadn't he said he was coming? She started to feel like she could finally forgive herself for something that was not, and never had been, her fault.

OLD TEMPERANCEVILLE
BY MIKE WATT

The old Kaufmann house had teeth and eyes. That's how the shattered windows looked to us kids. Had we known what our rocks would create, we would have left them at our feet. Now we had a demonic face at the end of our lane, staring out at us day and night. You couldn't hide from it anywhere on Bangor Street.

This was in the fall. Before Mr. Gimbal bought the house, but not too long after they dragged Crazy Annie Kaufmann through the door, paramedics on each frail arm, and stuffed her into the white ambulance. All up and down the block, you could hear her scream; you could see her scarecrow body through her nightgown, barely registering the snowflakes landing on her ice-paper skin. From my window I saw the white scars on the inside of her left arm, caught in the streetlight. Where she'd tried to scrub the numbers away with steel wool. My brother told me that when he was my age, she used to charge kids a quarter to lift her sleeve and see the fish-scale flesh and the very vague blue ink symbols floating underneath.

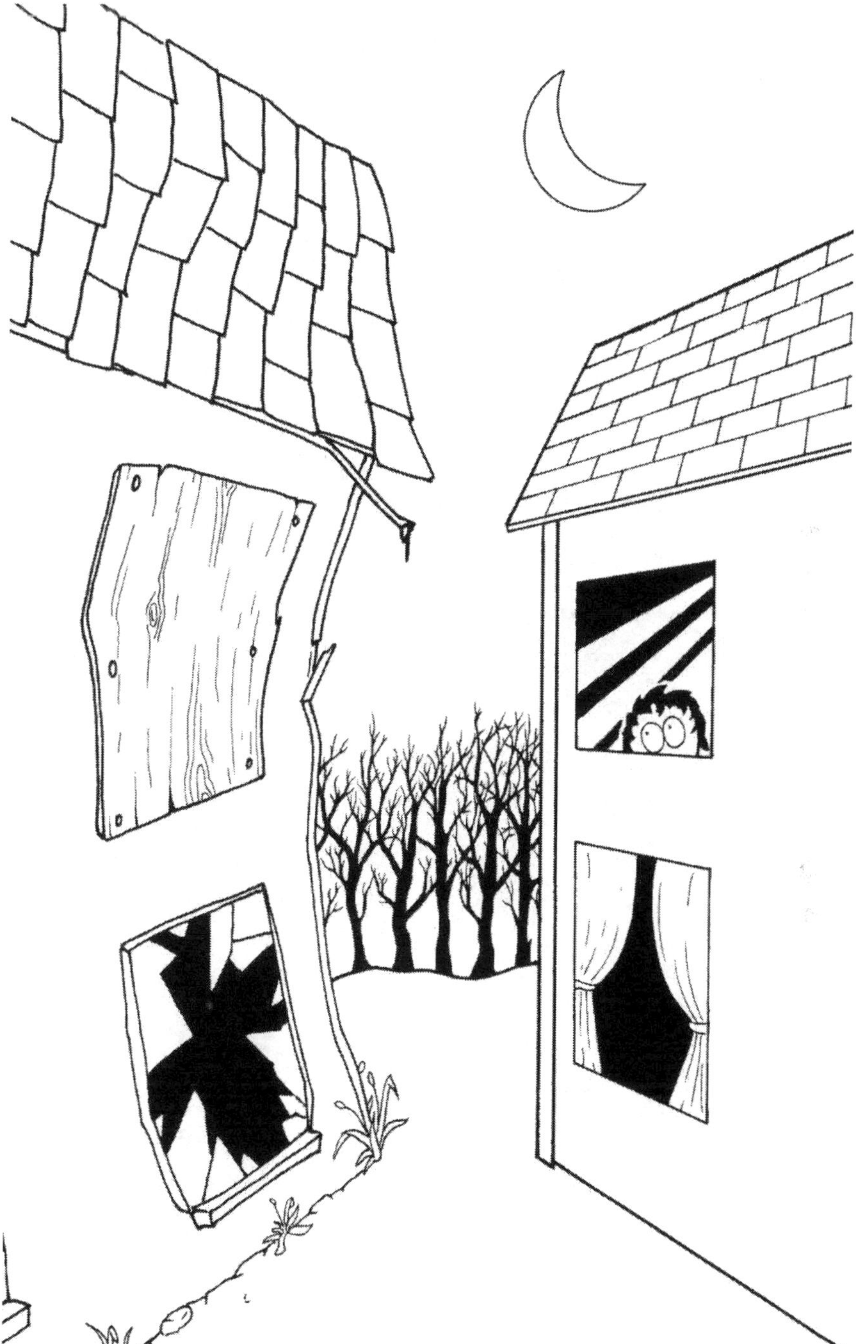

For almost a year, the old Kaufmann house stood empty, its Satan window-face keeping watch. To the older kids in Temperanceville, the empty dwelling proved too much temptation. Late at night, while fathers up and down the street labored for the dying railroad, the teenagers would brave the guardian's stare and violate the threshold with their music and spray paint and condoms and need for stupid destruction.

When Mr. Gimbal finally came along, there wasn't a wall standing unblemished by painted profanity or holes bashed by hammer or boot heel. His first duty was to the windows, clearing the sharpest shards from the panes, nailing planks over the voids, shutting out the rest of town.

My family lived next door, our house separated from the Kaufmann place by little more than a muddy alley leading to a ravine behind the houses. This alley, yielding maybe six feet of space between my bedroom window and the boarded-up blinded eye across the way, was to my mind a no-man's land, some unspoken line in the sand between our house and the Kaufmann place. Before Mr. Gimbal, that hollow eye held the terror of Hell for me. When Freddy first leaned over my sill and sent his baseball through the glass, it was like he'd shattered some protective spell. As if he'd lifted the house's cloudy lid, allowing it to stare directly at me any time I was home. On windy nights, the gauzy curtains would escape their dusty room and seem to stream like tears, or ghostly arms reaching for me.

This was a few years before Mrs. Arnett shot her

husband and the twins and then herself, but not too long after Mr. Gimbal moved in. After the boards went up over the windows the new landlord became invisible to Temperanceville, but not unknown to us. It was easy to tell when he was home—whether I was in my bedroom or at the other end of Bangor St.—because of the near-constant sounds of hammering, sawing, drilling. Ceaseless sounds of construction. With dad at the rail yard, my mother at the diner, my brother in the war, I was the only one kept awake by the noise. Mr. Gimbal would run his band saw late into the night. Sometimes it sounded like a woman, screaming.

Mr. Gimbal had a lot of girlfriends. The number of women who went in and out of his home added scandal to the neighborhood's frustration with his introverted nature, compounding the distrust and the dislike. Mrs. Grabowski once took a freshly made pie to him in the middle of the afternoon, and she never got past the porch. The big project taking shape behind his front door remained a mystery. This was before Mrs. Grabowski's daughter got sick, but not too long after her husband had left her finally and for good.

One night that fall, a storm came through. I watched it kick up the leaves, swirl them around with the dust and other debris, sweeping loose crud from one end of the street to the other. The sharp smell of electric current mixed and mingled with the familiar aromas of autumn, the crispness of the air chasing away the hotter summer temperatures as the days grew shorter and shorter. The storm tore shingles and siding from every house on the block, unmoored several boards from the Kaufmann house's upstairs windows. Somehow, the window across from mine, my enemy, avoided destruction, but from then on the wind would rattle the loose planks like keys of a dead piano.

When Mr. Gimbal pried nails from the hardwood floors, it sounded like babies shrieking at nightmares. One night, a tiny white hand waved at me from the gap between the rattling boards. The next night the house seemed closer to mine. The alley had shrunk during the day. This was after Freddy's drunk dad took a crowbar to his boss's windshield, finding it unexpectedly parked in his driveway. It was just before Mr. Gimbal began finding dead animals nailed to his front door. Just after someone spray-painted the Star of David on the side of his shed. Everyone sort of knew it was Mr. John Tracy. They'd had a fight about religion at Mrs. Ewen's yard sale. By the end of the week, Gimbal had it painted over without a word to anyone.

Maybe it was because Halloween was so close, but our fascination with Mr. Gimbal and the old Kaufmann house only grew stronger each night, as the streetlights switched on earlier and earlier. When you're a kid, Halloween is a special time, a forbidden time that only kids recognize. The anticipation for trick 'r treating mounted, kept us shifting in our seats at school. As the holiday approached, it seemed like everyone's nerves stretched tighter, waiting for an alarm that never seemed to sound.

Freddy said his old man saw two barrels of sulfuric acid sitting just inside Mr. Gimbal's garage. Right next to them was a woman's shoe. But even Freddy admitted that his dad had been drunk that night, like nearly every other night. By the weekend, the hospital released Freddy's mother with a wired-shut jaw and Freddy swore he was going to kill his sonofabitch father and burn the whole neighborhood to the ground. This was before he finally did.

Our other friend, Donny, who lived across from Freddy, didn't turn up for dinner one night. He always talked about running away, because his mom's new boyfriend didn't like him. Or liked him too much, I guess. It took us years to figure out what the adults were whispering when they thought we weren't in earshot. At the time kids just understood that some adults couldn't be lived with.

Before school finally let out for the weekend, they found Donny's bike in the ravine behind our place. By this time, the Kaufman house was close enough to brush with my fingertips, with me barely leaning out of my window. The alley was too narrow for Donny to fit down walking, much less on his bike. And with the big fence Gimbal put up around the lot, the alley was the only path from the street to the ravine. Freddy said that Donny probably wanted us to think he was dead, so that no one would come looking for him. I didn't think Donny was that creative, but they didn't find Donny's body, and we didn't want to talk about a different explanation. This was before we finally moved, but after the Marines brought my mother a folded American flag.

I know it wasn't a dream. I woke up to the light and hiss

of the TV station signing off to static, casting inkblot patterns all over the room. I'd started sleeping with my father's .22 pistol under my bed, returning it to the shoebox in his closet every morning before he came home. But I knew if I made a move for it, it would be the last thing I ever did.

So I stayed frozen in bed, terrified, because the Kaufmann window was bare inches from my face.

The rear of the Kaufmann house was *inside* my house, both occupying the same space. If I leaned forward I would tumble through the boards, now spread open like a woman's legs, with blackness yawning beyond. I would fall through that window and wind up in both that dusty room and my own at the same time. If I wound up in that room I'd be able to see what Mr. Gimbal had been building all this time. I'd know why a shredded patch of Donny's jacket had blown onto my pillow the morning before.

Instead of leaning forward I reared back. As far against my headboard as I could, putting blankets and pillows between me and that glaring and beckoning black eye and the blinking, chattering wood plank lids. This was before the fire and many, many years before my upstairs neighbor, a prostitute, hurled her infant from the roof of our apartment building. In hindsight, the sudden wet, strangled cry upon impact I heard echoed the noise I heard behind the boards of the Kaufmann window, just inches from my bed and getting closer. This is exactly when I knew that I must *never* know what made that noise.

In the morning, my father found me standing at the

opposite end of our street, barefoot and in my pajamas, his gun dangling from my fingers. When he picked me up, I barely acknowledged him. Doctors later diagnosed me as a 'somnambulist'. I will admit I was surprised to see that the Kaufmann house had returned to its place across the alley. More or less. The window was still close enough to touch without really leaning.

The second time they found me wandering like that was the night of the fire, as all of Temperanceville burned to ash, one house falling after another. That was another autumn, though.

After Freddy had had enough of his father, after his mother lost her left eye. Before Donny's body was found in the charred and blackened alley, stretched between our scorched houses as if he'd been leaping from one window to another. Before Freddy went to the hospital and then prison for the rest of his childhood. Before the railroad folded and we had to finally move. Before we'd heard that Mr. Gimbal had died in a car accident on Christmas Eve. But long after the first tortured shriek of pried-up nails and dead infants echoed in my ears.

THE JOROGUMO'S DAUGHTER
BY K.Z. MORANO

"Chloe, um, you kind of look like shit," Tara told me after History.

It was true. My hair had turned dry and brittle and my complexion was unnaturally pale. I hadn't slept in days, and I was fully conscious of my gross panda eyes. And lately, I'd been suffering from some mysterious malaise. Apart from the insomnia, I experienced symptoms of fatigue, lack of appetite, and strangely, some unexplainable weight gain. With luck, I wouldn't need to worry about my costume for the forthcoming annual Autumn Ball. The theme was Beast and I thought I looked beastly enough.

Ms. Thomas, my English teacher, said that autumn is that time of the year when the Earth begins to unclothe herself, seeking respite from all the beauty and color, so she can breathe. For awhile, she endures a brief period of plainness until she's ready to be beautiful again. I was like: Way to go, Earth. Being so beautiful that you actually beg to have a break from it all... I wished that I could say that the same thing was happening to me, but the truth was I'd always been a Plain Jane. And I thought, if I ever got the chance to be pretty, I'd never want to "seek respite" from it at all.

It wasn't until my hair started falling out in clumps that I decided to drop by the school clinic. Miss Mabery gave me some vitamins and suggested the use of a milder shampoo. She even recommended some expensive moisturizer for my dry, flaking skin. There was no way that I could afford a jar of that stuff. I had long suspected the school nurse's most outstanding, and perhaps her *only* qualification, for the job was her clinically white smile and the manner in which her breasts pushed, alert and attentive, against her tight uniform. Both Tara and I thought that it was criminal to let her walk about in a school filled with pre and post-pubescent girls. As if catching the boys' attention wasn't hard enough. We concluded Miss Mabery was sent there to make certain that high school indeed became the living hell that it was meant to be, particularly for girls like me.

"Out of the way, hobbit."

I looked up to see Margot Mistral's flawless face and modelesque frame towering above me. I moved aside but still, that didn't stop her from bumping against me. There was a chorus of giggles from Margot's minions as my glasses clattered onto the floor. One of them scoffed at the newsboy cap I was wearing. I added an assortment of hats to my wardrobe in order to conceal the minute bald patches on my scalp. I was shorter than the average ninth grader. I thought it was probably due to my half-Asian ancestry, though I had never met my mother. My father refused to talk about her. I didn't know anything about her except that she committed suicide when I was a baby.

Margot Mistral was everything I was not. She was tall, beautiful, popular... Okay, so maybe I was smarter than her, but she was dating a senior. Not just any senior. She was dating Ash Akerman. I hated that my life seemed like a stupid teenage television series with all the stupid stereotypes and none of the magical endings where the shy girl gets a makeover, and the guy falls in love with her, and the bitchy villain gets her utterly humiliating comeuppance. Well, at least I had Tara, my BFF. Ours was an enduring sandbox love. Though lately, I hadn't been completely honest with her.

It wasn't just the loss of sleep and hair and appetite that was bothering me. My skin also seemed to be... shedding. Every morning, I'd find huge flakes of papery flesh on my sheets. I spent extra minutes in the shower scrubbing off the dead skin cells and moisturizing as best as I can. I loathed how the pieces of molted skin would get stuck to my fingers.

I didn't bother telling dad about these changes. His mind was too preoccupied with work and with paying the bills. Besides, teenage bodily changes were hardly matters I wished to discuss with my father. He'd tried to talk to me once about my period and tampons and stuff. It was a total fail. I loved him to pieces but since then, I had vowed to spare the both of us from all that awkwardness.

Besides, I didn't dislike *all* the changes. In time, I realized I looked better with a little meat on me. Soon, I noticed my body was filling out in all the right places. I realized, much to my satisfaction, I had grown a pair of breasts. Maybe they weren't like Miss Mabery's, but for the first time in my life, I actually had boobs. Yay! My hips also seemed rounder, my butt slightly bigger. My skin continued to self-exfoliate and soon, my complexion began to clear up. Silky strands grew rapidly from the bald spots on my scalp, replacing the rioting raven hair.

I convinced myself I was simply a late bloomer and that I was finally growing up. Still, that did not explain my suddenly perfect vision that forced me to ditch my eyeglasses. As thrilled as I was that I was suddenly turning a few heads, I couldn't help but suspect that something was very, very wrong.

~

Maybe it was hormones. Maybe God, or guardian angels, or fairy godmothers were real. Maybe I had unleashed some dormant teenage superpower. Maybe I simply hadn't been aware of my true potentials. Whatever the reason was, I turned almost overnight from a total loser to one of the most popular girls in school.

My movements seemed more confident, my posture more graceful, my reflexes quicker. I was never the athletic type but my body somehow developed this extraordinary agility. My senses were stronger, my memory highly improved. I turned from good student to stellar pupil with no extra effort. Like a sponge, I absorbed every lesson, every book, and every conversation down to the tiniest, most tedious detail. I had no idea where I got the energy from. I could feel the power like gasoline stored inside my stomach, constantly refilling itself. I felt almost invincible.

Something else was changing... something inside me. I seemed more driven, more daring, more likely to say and do things that I would've never done before. I was never the impulsive type, and I was used to my instincts failing me about 97% of the time, but somewhere along the way, I started giving in to spontaneous urges and in the process, learned to stop doubting myself. When I tried out for the cheerleading team, I totally killed it. Since it was gradually becoming obvious to everyone that *the new girl* was better than her, it was only proper for Margot to invite me into her circle. To be honest, they terrified me—those girls with their designer handbags and acid tongues, but at the same time, it was everything I had ever wanted. Except, of course, that that meant I had to stop hanging out with Tara.

It wasn't like I ditched her for them or anything. She made the choice for me. She was being so uncool about the whole Margot thing. She said that Margot made her feel uncomfortable and that she couldn't be trusted. I was like: "Duh. Margot makes *everyone* uncomfortable." I told her to stop being such a hater, that I wasn't stupid and it's not like I really trusted Margot and that if she really was my best friend, she'd be happy for me. Tara was being so unfair. Then just like that, she stopped replying to my texts. So I quit bothering her.

My breakup with Tara hurt me more than I dared to

admit to myself or to my dad. However, there was one particular breakup that really made my school year. Margot broke up with Ash Akerman. Or was it the other way around? Anyway, it didn't really matter because Ash asked me to be his date for the Autumn Ball. *Oh. My. Effin'. God.* But even then, all I could think of was how I wished that Tara was there to help me choose my outfit and fix my hair and just... be there for me. I didn't know why but I ended up settling for a sexy spider costume. I was looking for something that screamed femme fatale and the body-hugging, black and purple leather number that sprouted extra limbs and emphasized my new cleavage seemed perfect.

~

The gym was crawling with creatures that ranged from weird to WTF. With students wearing costumes that were more slutty than scary, it felt more like a BDSM club than a school dance. After a couple of dances, Ash asked me if I wanted to sneak out. He took me to Fat Bob's for burgers. We split the bill. He talked about himself most of the time and I listened raptly with doglike admiration. I found myself wishing that relationships could thrive on swag alone. There we were in his car, parked in some deserted place. Ash had zombie makeup all over his face. He leaned over to kiss me and I felt my heart become inflated with proportionate amounts of desire and fear. It was my first kiss. He was gentle at first, his tongue both tentative and teasing. I remained unaware of the hand that had been sliding up my spine until I felt the faint snap of my suddenly unfastened corset.

"No," I whispered, recoiling instinctively.

If he heard, he gave no indication. His kisses became rougher. His hands crept inside my clothes to pinch my nipples and squeeze my breasts. I could feel his hard-on pressing against me.

"No," I repeated, pushing him away more forcefully.

"Fucking tease." He snarled, his handsome features contorted with fury, the zombie face paint making him seem grotesque and terrifying. Then just as quickly, his face melted into its usual cool countenance. "You better put out, Chloe," he coaxed, his voice dripping with malice. "Because if you don't, I'll tell everyone what a real slut you are."

He let out a harsh chuckle. His breath was hot against my face. It reeked of Fat Bob's chili burgers and onion rings. In an instant, all my expectations left me like helium bursting out of a punctured balloon. It was a ridiculous threat but I had a feeling that it had worked for him before. At that moment, my entire body grew paralyzed with fear.

"I'll be gentle. Promise," he said. His rotting zombie mouth covered my trembling lips as he pulled down his pants.

I felt the bile rise in my throat—bitter, burning, and inevitable. I was so nervous that I vomited into his mouth.

"What the fu..." He gurgled as he pulled away. Then his eyes grew wide, so wide that I thought his entire head would explode. It didn't. Instead, Ash clutched his stomach, his face twisted in a terrible grimace. Then he reached between his thighs. When his hand came away, his shaking fingers were all bloody and covered with slimy pulped flesh. I watched, my fear magnifying with each second, as blood and what I assumed to be his liquefied entrails swirled down his legs.

I struggled to get the door open and rushed out of the car. I was only vaguely aware of the sharp ripping sound that one of my fake spider limbs made as Ash desperately clung to it. I backed away, ever so slowly, unable to tear my gaze away from the nightmarish scene. He crawled towards me, dragged his body out of the car and onto the pavement. His face, his body, they appeared to be shrinking in front of me until he looked less and less like Ash Akerman and more and more like a real animated corpse. He tried to scream, his mouth a black bottomless pit on his emaciated face, but no sound came out of the tongueless cavity. So I opened my mouth and screamed for the both of us.

At that moment, I was nothing but a screaming bundle of nerves. My brain exploded within my skull. I felt myself swelling and swelling, expanding until the exhausted fibers of my skin started snapping. I felt myself unraveling, one fiber at a time. I was no longer me. I was nothing but loosely connected ganglia—dividing, multiplying, scattering. Then I was everywhere—hundreds and thousands of little Chloes—crazed, curious, creeping through the pavement, then cutting pathways through Ash's flesh.

I entered his body through every cavity, an entire colony

of me, all conscious and crawling and throbbing with life. I was beneath his skin, burrowing, breathing... I was *inside* him, plumping his body, filling him up the way chaff and sawdust fills a mummified corpse. It was like an orgy of me taking place inside a sarcophagus of his hollow, lifeless body. Then every tiny crawling Chloe—every fine furry limb, every one of my thousands of pinhead eyes—exploded in ecstasy.

~

A few days later, the police came to ask some questions. I told them I went with Ash to the dance and then we had dinner afterwards. I told them of how he had ended the date abruptly when I refused to put out. They seemed satisfied with my story, even nodding sympathetically from time to time. They were certain that his disappearance had something to do with the ample amounts of a new street drug they had discovered inside his room.

My days as a popular girl had been short-lived. I became quiet and withdrawn. I stopped answering calls and attending parties. I realized I couldn't care less about what others thought of me. Not while there were too many weird things happening. I remembered walking home that night, limping and a bit disoriented, having no idea at all what happened to Ash's corpse. I was still pretty shaken but apart from the shock and confusion, there was something else too.

I became aware of every single cell of my body. My skin was constantly itching. I could feel phantom spiders crawling just underneath the pruritic flesh, threatening to break free, like gelled pus boiling beneath a zit that's about to pop. I could feel them frolicking inside my skull, their miniscule bodies hissing in a sustained susurrus as they writhed and rubbed against each other.

Tara started talking to me again, telling me she was worried. I stayed away. I couldn't tell her the truth. It was never my intention to hurt anyone and though I would never dare hurt Tara, at that moment, I just couldn't trust myself.

~

I found the letter one night while I was leafing through one of the old baby albums Dad had kept hidden inside the cellar. I came down there in an attempt to forget about the present, to momentarily dwell in the past. The paper was creased and yellowed, frayed at the edges. Inkblots and stained fingerprints peppered the page as though someone had kept reading and re-reading the note, wetting the fragile paper with briny beads of sweat or tears. My heart hammered against my ribcage like an insect's wings beating against its glass prison. Somehow, I knew the letter was from my mother. The indecipherable message had been hand-written in Japanese so I went online to find a way to translate it. The rough translation was:

I was a spider who wanted to become human. I have lived 400 years to acquire this form. Above all things, I wanted love. I waited again for 100 years to find it. Now I can rest at last. Thank you, my love.

A few more online searches led me to the Jorōgumo, also

known as the "whore spider". According to Japanese folklore, when a rare spider lives up to 400 years old, it acquires deific powers and may take the form of a human. Most Jorōgumo assume the shape of a lovely woman skilled in playing the *biwa*. They would seduce men with their music and their charms and then devour them for sustenance. There were tales about Jorōgumo who fell in love with mortal men and mortal men who fell in love with them, despite knowing their true nature. There was also one about an exorcism done by a Buddhist priest to cast the evil spider spirit away from a young man whom the binding spider bride had ensorcelled. There were ancient paintings depicting the prostitute spider as a creature with a woman's face and torso and a giant arachnid's opisthosoma, spinnerets, and eight limbs. Some regard the Jorōgumo as a demon; some call it an evil spirit, while there are some who consider the half-woman, half-spider creature as a protecting deity.

~

I found him in his study, engrossed in paperwork. I dropped my mother's suicide note on his desk. My father's face darkened.

"Where did you get this?" he asked, but the question was futile. He grabbed the piece of paper and shoved it inside the drawer. "Chloe, sweetheart, what's past is pas—"

"I killed him." The words were like speeding bullets—deadly, irreversible—shooting out of my mouth and boring holes into my father's heart. "Daddy, I killed Ash."

For a moment, he was speechless, his face blanched white in terror. Terror of what? Of me? I couldn't bear the thought.

"Daddy," I sobbed. "What am I?"

~

Demon, evil spirit, or protecting deity... I realized that it was entirely up to me which one I was going to be. Mother was a demon because that's what she chose to become. She was a murderess, a whore, a cannibalistic beast, wearing women's bodies like flesh suits and selling her love to men who would later fill her belly. She did all of these things with no other purpose than to sustain her youth and beauty. She took lives until she could no longer do it.

Perhaps the worst of all her faults was that she was a terrible mother. She fell in love with my father and she couldn't handle it. She spared his life so that she could pass her egg sac to him and then flung herself into her watery grave in what she thought was a noble act of sacrifice. She'd rather die than change. She preferred to drown than to face a life that was other than what she had always known. My mother didn't know anything about sacrifice. She understood nothing about responsibility. But I knew what I was meant to be. I watched the Spiderman movie over and over and the words became a mantra to me: *With great power comes great responsibility.* Okay, so perhaps Voltaire may have said it first, but I liked to believe the film was speaking to me. And while I may not be the ideal teenage superhero, well, at least I was willing to do my part in making the world a better place.

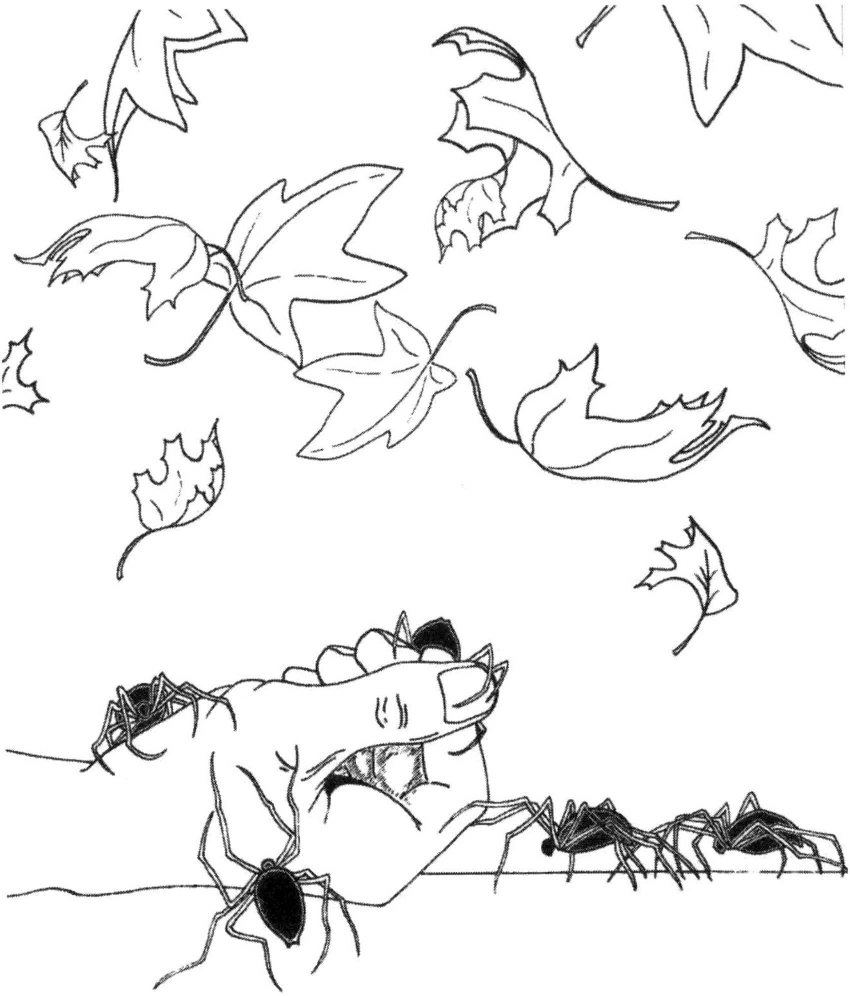

~

Taylor Hayter took me out on a romantic picnic by the lake. He was handsome and a lot older than me. The gravid moon cast ghostly reflections on the water, making the surface shimmer like silver spider webs.

In the cool autumn wind, the semi-naked trees shuddered and golden leaves swirled around us like expired butterflies. He leaned over. Panicked spasms stirred inside my gut. I closed my eyes and my lips parted as his mouth hovered just above mine. I held my breath for what felt like the longest time until my lungs were aching, begging to collapse. Then with a sudden stroke of boldness, I rose to meet his lips.

My timidity gradually abandoned my body and in its place formed a red wall of hatred. I could feel the disgusting dinner that we had rising up my throat—Gruyère cheese, Greek salad, chocolate truffles, expensive wine. He even bought me flowers. How could he not? He made loads of money selling packets of the new street drug to kids in school. A certain part of me believed in the honesty of his feelings for me. Still, I had a grave responsibility.

He pulled away and for awhile, the startled expression on his face mirrored mine. He tried to say something, his staccato speech choking itself out of his mouth as my venom trickled down the back of his throat. Then, like a sex-starved maniac, I unbuckled his belt, then pulled down his pants. This time, I knew better than to just stand back and watch in horror.

I crawled towards him, my proboscis-like tongue unraveling. The stars leered like a constellation of voyeuristic eyes as they watched me make love to his body. Soon, the human Chloe crumbled and the picnic blanket was covered by thousands of tiny Chloes, clambering clots of flesh—eight-legged and many-eyed—crawling inside the orbits of Taylor's sunken eyes, entering his ears, his nostrils, creating new orifices until his body was bursting with me.

I lingered inside him for a little while, basking in the afterglow, a bit reluctant to let go. As I lay inside him, I recalled an article that said that autumn is spider season. During this time of the year, arachnids invade human homes in search of a place to stay and to mate during the winter. Suddenly, I understood my mother, understood the addictive sensations of invading a person's body and feeding on his vigor. At that moment, I knew the whole superhero thing was merely an excuse, and that even without the just cause that I had thrust upon myself, I would still be doing this if only for the sheer pleasure it brings.

Even then I knew what I was—a myriad of thinly veiled monstrosities, ancient and hungry, hiding inside a teenager's body. I was a Jorōgumo's daughter, eggs passed from body to body throughout the centuries. My body was nothing but a haunted vessel and peering from behind the lenses of my eyes were thousands of baby spiders, each of them waiting for their 400th birthday... waiting to break free.

THE TWISTED END OF VERNON BOGGS
BY BROOKE WARRA

They came knocking at his ever-locked door and showed him the papers, while their smiles slithered across their skeleton jaws like hungry serpents disguised as human flesh. They offered him a bit of coin for a bit of a dilapidated house. A house, he whined, he had not set one moldy foot from in thirty years. They tried to peek in, tried to put shiny shoes in the doorway and nudge the outside in. He held fast the doorknob, reached one warty hand out, glared with one scab-addled eye at their repulsed faces and took their stinking papers before he slammed the door. They gave him no choice. The bulldozer would come whether he stayed or went.

He would take nothing with him, he decided. He would go deep into the forest where he could lay his matted head down in the moss and the muck and not be moved.

So Vernon Boggs fled into the autumn night, achingly

1428

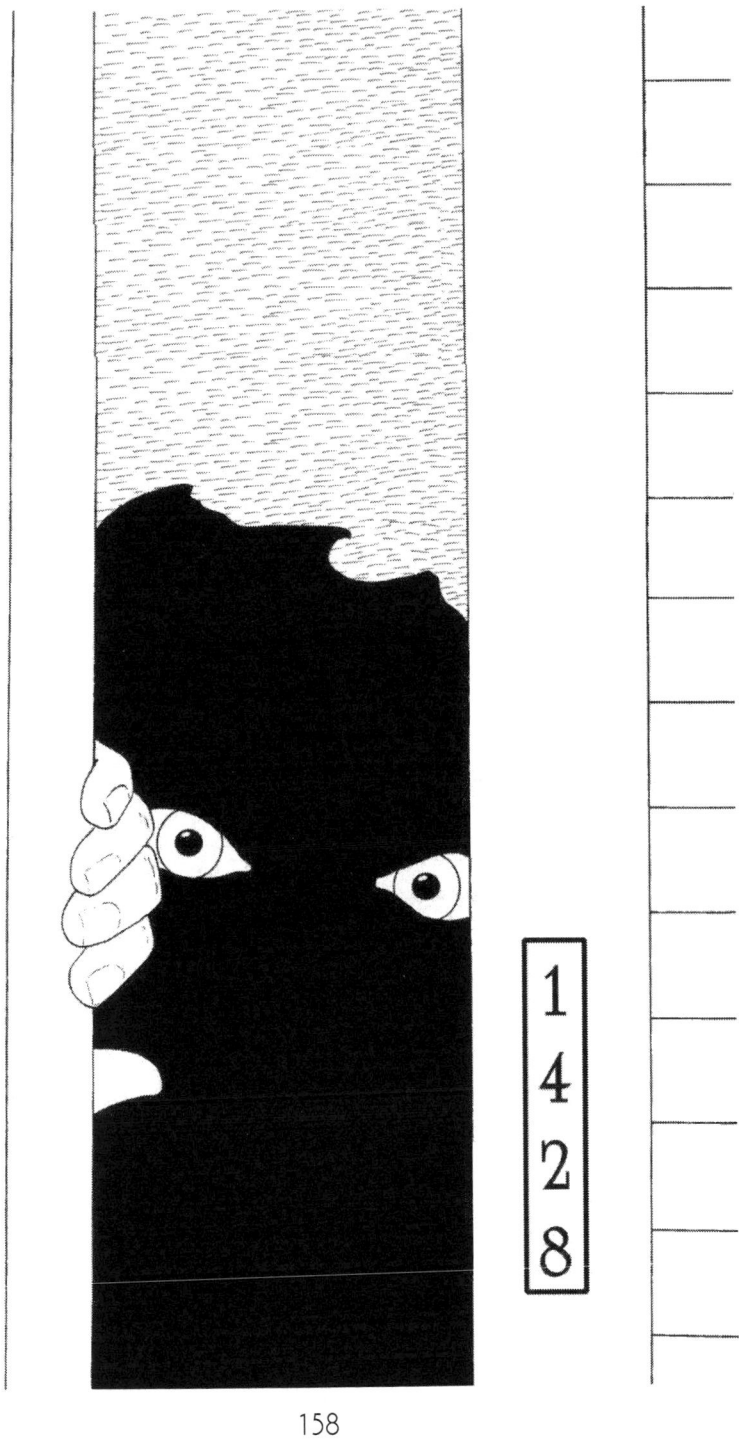

slow on his little-used legs, bent at the waist from decades of rocking in his favorite chair among the dust that had settled around him. A mist of cobwebs drifted behind him as he trudged through the thickets. The spiders that had made a home in his hair dropped from him and darted into the underbrush to find new, less shifty homes. He resented their treachery.

As he watched the creatures scuttle away on fragile bones across the rotting forest floor, he wondered if the shiny-shoed people had found mother in the cellar yet. That first terrible traitor who had conspired to uproot him from their happy home.

"You're grown now, Vernon," she had said. She had been splitting fire wood for the winter ahead. Every fall of the axe upon the wet stump made a sound like splitting flesh.

Squish.

"You should have a family."

Squish.

"You should meet a nice girl."

Squish.

He'd grabbed a hold of his head. "Can't you hear that?!"

"Hear what?" She continued to chop at the meat of the stump. "I'm just saying, Vernon, you can't stay here for—"

Squelch.

That last sound had been the brick in Vernon's hand sinking into her skull. He would not leave this house if he could help it. And neither would she.

She still lay where he had left her among the shadows that had hidden his sin. There had been a flurry of scritchy-scratch noises that had taken most of her away. They would find the bones, though. The bones were always leftover after you crushed things with heavy hands.

He decided it didn't matter now and pressed on, dragging first one jelly-fleshed foot and then the other in his sluggish descent into the woods. Eventually he found a boggy little cluster of trees to settle down in. He laid his aching body along the mossy ground and proceeded to burrow into it. At last, no one and nothing could move him. No glossy-suited snakes in people's skin could find him here. He sighed heavily with relief as the dirt settled over the soft yolks of his eyes.

When he slept, he did not fear the sounds of the animals. The old home had been a teeming nest of vermin that skittered across him as he slumbered. For this same reason, he did not fear hunger in his new home. He did not fear thirst as he scooped handfuls of festering, wooly water into his decaying mouth.

What he did fear was the creaking. At first it came from the sounds of the trees, their low mournful groans as the wind passed through and shook their motionless bodies into unwanted movement. They lolled their heads and twisted their arms in protest as the gale pressed down upon them. All the time, they moaned painfully. And he understood. But soon the creaking ceased to come from outside of himself. A rasping filled his ears no matter which way he turned or how he covered them or filled them with bits of moss. Days and days went by and he thought he would be driven mad by the infernal scraping inside his head. Before that could happen, though, a new thing began.

He woke to an exquisite pain that snaked through his idle limbs, the creaking inside growing to an earsplitting hum he could not ignore, if he had ever been able to before. He held up a gnarled hand to his filmy eyes and saw with great fascination the knuckles of his fingers and the knobs of his wrist bones protruding and gray through his skin. The veins in his hands and down his arms were rivers of some black sludge. He watched as they pulsed underneath his flesh, seemingly growing wider with each passing moment. The ooze flared through every capillary in his body, down to his toes which bowed in remonstration to the invading matter.

He desperately struggled as his flesh flaked away in curls. It turned white, then scaly, then wispy, and crumbled off. He watched it harden in patches as elsewhere in him there were a great many snapping noises. His body was thrust upward by the force of all his limbs being contorted at once. His hands shot out high above his head, as they had not been since the day he'd brought down the brick upon his mother's skull when she had, with her back turned to him, mentioned in passing that he might like to go out in the world and make a life of his own. The tips of his fingers were the first to rupture. Bright green shoots grew from his nailbeds and sought the daylight that filtered through the canopy of trees above. His kneecaps were the next to burst. Spindly tentacles whipped into the air, sought the marshy ground and plunged into it with their spiky ends. His body became a spiral, stretching taller as each vertebra popped and separated, his pink flesh tearing open to reveal knotted gray scales underneath.

There was a final snapping sound as the last of his bones cracked and his flesh split wide and fell away.

From then on, his days would be filled with that ever-groaning, that always-creaking, that infernal hum of a million moaning fibers each time the breeze caressed his new body. There Vernon Boggs stood forever, suffering every season as his leaves curled and turned to brittle gold, fluttering away from him to the mossy floor. Birds would nest. Vermin would gnaw at his flesh. And Vernon Boggs would let out an internal, eternal scream only the forest could hear.

THE BALFOUR WITCH
BY TAWNY KIPPHORN

There stands a house in Autumn Falls
Where the purest evil lives in the walls
And if you dare enter the home on Carmine Lane
She'll destroy your mind and make you insane.

Legend says its grounds are cursed
By the Balfour Witch to quench her thirst
For the blood of all who inhabit the place
From whence she had once fallen from grace.

It was the year of sixteen-seventy-one
When the dawn of October bestowed a son
To the Balfour Witch, then called Rosalee
Filled to the brim with such joy was she.

Until one night came the sound of yelling
From a voice just outside her little dwelling
Rosalee caught the scent of a blazing fire
And through her window saw a man next to a pyre.

"You will burn, witch!" shouted the man. "You'll rot in hell!"
To escape she tried but down the stairs she fell.
Down her legs pools of vermilion did run
As she screamed in agony at the loss of her son.

Into her home the man barreled in
About to commit the ultimate sin
Dragged her he did by her locks of red
And threw her onto her fiery bed.

An ungodly shriek rang through the air
Transfixing all with a bone-chilling scare
And just as she was believed to be dead
All became plagued with a sense of dread.

Everyone feared what would be in store
For the Balfour Witch had risen once more
As she recited her spell as loud as she could
The guilty dropped dead right where they stood.

"I curse this land now and forever!
No one escapes, not now, not ever!"
As time went on and centuries passed
Her curse remained forever cast.

The only way to escape her wrath
Is to follow in her murderous path
Craving the blood she needs to sustain
The blood of innocents so she will remain.

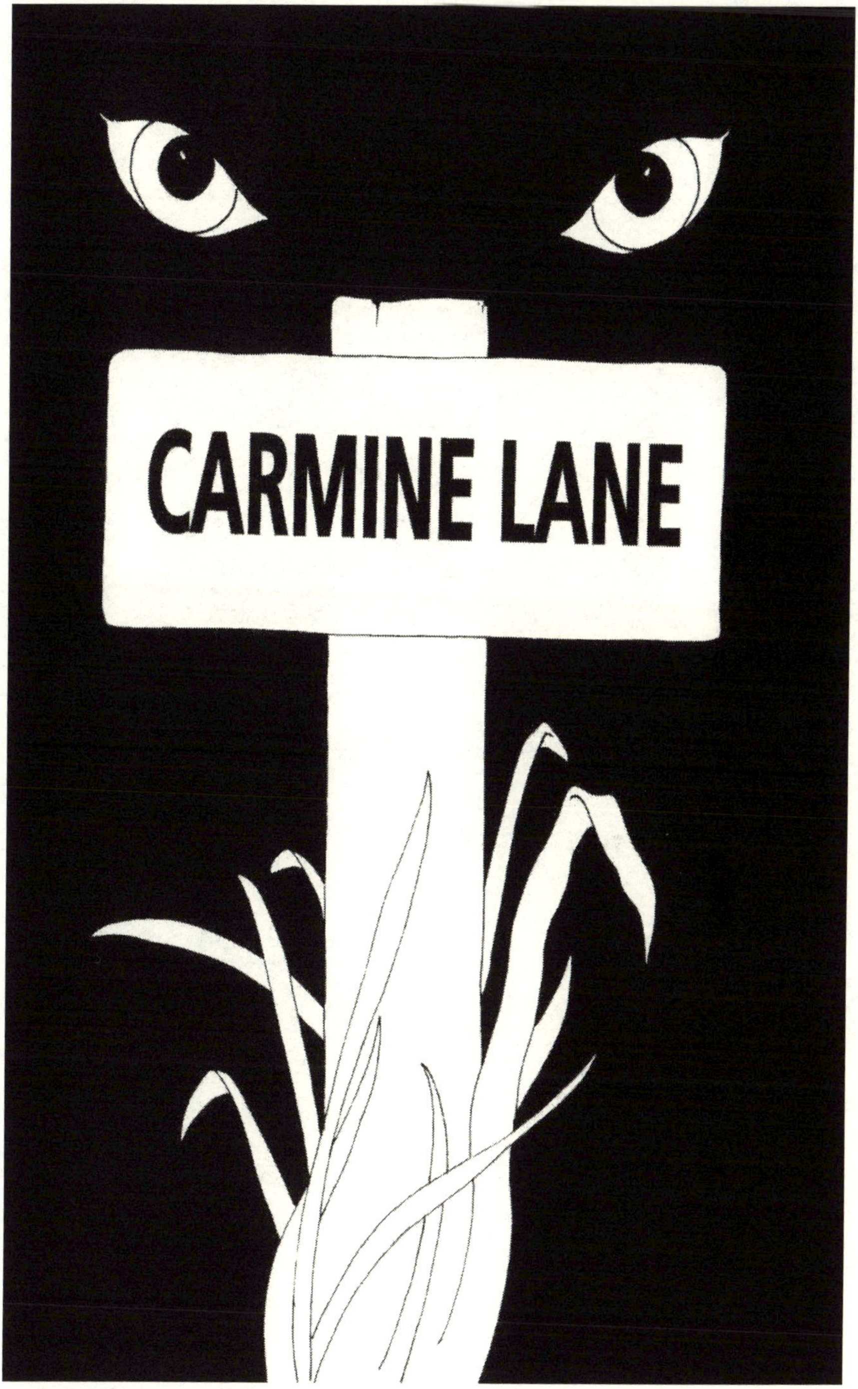
CARMINE LANE

But to this coin lies another side
From a guilty conscience one cannot hide
For once you commit this violent act
You kill yourself to fulfill the pact.

The pact in which you've unknowingly made
With your own life to her you've paid
Only the brave dare to visit this home
Whence the Balfour Witch continues to roam.

Here today in modern times
She's the reason for these crimes.
Forever we mourn the lives she's taken
As every October the witch awakens.

If you visit these grounds you must beware
Of the Balfour Witch that lurks in despair.
Hidden within her haven of pain
The house that sits on Carmine Lane.

ABOUT THE AUTHORS

Gerri Leen lives in Northern Virginia and originally hails from Seattle. She has stories and poems published by Daily Science Fiction, Escape Pod, Grimdark, Athena's Daughters 2 and others. She is editing an anthology, *A Quiet Shelter There*, which will benefit homeless animals and is due out in 2015 from Hadley Rille Books. See more at http://www.gerrileen.com.

J. Tonzelli is a writer, film journalist, and Halloween enthusiast who currently resides in rural South Jersey. He is the author of *The End of Summer: Thirteen Tales of Halloween* and also co-authors a series for younger readers called "Fright Friends Adventures" under the shared pen name, The Blood Brothers. The first book, *The House on Creep Street*, is available now, and the next adventure is currently in press. When not obsessively checking the weather report for thunderstorms, he continues his appreciation for all things creepy while making too many jokes about skeletons. He loves autumn, abandoned buildings, the supernatural, and films by John Carpenter. You can read more of J. Tonzelli's short fiction, as well as his musings on film, at his website: www.JTonzelli.com

Scarlett R. Algee's work has appeared in Morpheus Tales, the *Cthulhu Haiku* anthologies, and Sanitarium Magazine. When not performing her duties as an avatar of Nyarlathotep, she lives in the wilds of Tennessee with a Hound of Tindalos cleverly disguised as a beagle. Find her online at sralgee.wordpress.com.

John Kiste was fed a steady diet of Poe and plots from Universal horror movies as bedtime stories while growing up and has been writing creepy tales ever since. He won The Times Reporter's Halloween story contest three times and had one of his ghoulish fairy tales published in the recent anthology, *Modern Grimmoire*. In his spare time, he performs a one-man show as Edgar Allan Poe throughout northeastern Ohio. He married the love of his life, Lonna, thirty-four years ago on Halloween, which makes this holiday a monster deal each year in their Ohio home where they have boasted 300 trick-or-treaters. Their cat Boo is black, of course—and you may have heard of their daughter...

It was a dark and stormy night when **Julia Benally** escaped the Whiteriver Indian Hospital alive. She's spent half of her existence in the Mexican Barrios of Mesa, Arizona and the other half on the Fort Apache Reservation. Julia enjoys swinging her nunchucks—unless she smacks herself, but she hasn't knocked herself out yet. She enjoys hunting, fishing and the delicate art of cross stitching. She enjoys dancing, but only when no one is looking. She's a great soprano until she has to sing in public. What she most enjoys is writing. She's been doing it since she was eight but got her first real publication with Sanitarium Magazine. Since then, she's been featured in Snapping Twig Magazine and has upcoming works in both. Recently, Julia has finished her first novel, *Pariahs*, which is a Dark Fantasy that takes place within an American Indian world.

Miracle Austin is a YA/NA cross-genre author. She's been writing ever since first hearing "Drive" by The Cars in junior high. Horror/suspense are her favorite genres, though her work is not limited to those genres. She enjoys writing diverse flashes and short stories, and she's completed her first forthcoming short story collection, the extremely eclectic *Boundless*, which requires minds to be open to the impossible and is a gumbo of themes, some light-hearted while others are much darker. She's currently working on her first novelette, *Doll*, and stand-alone novel, *Lonestar UnOrdinary Girl*, a supernatural tale with comedic elements. She resides in Texas with her family. Find her online at miracleaustin.com as well as on Facebook and Twitter.

Lee A. Forman is an author residing in the Hudson Valley, NY with his daughter and four cats. He's been a fan of horror literature and cinema since his fascination with the macabre began in childhood, watching old movies and reading every novel he could get his hands on. He's a third generation horror fan, starting with his grandfather who was a fan of the classic Hollywood monsters. He spends most of his time writing short fiction, reading, and hiking trails in the Catskill Mountains. In October 2014, he won 3rd place in the Writer's Carnival Short Story Contest hosted by Sanitarium Magazine, and in 2015, he was a competitor in David Wellington's Fear Project. He's currently writing a serialized novella titled, *Silence in the Willow Field*. For more information, a list of publications, and to read his web series, go to leeandrewforman.wordpress.com.

Living in the vast expanse of rural farmland east of Pittsburgh, Pennsylvania with his three pets, two sons, and wife (just one wife...), **Daniel Weaver** is an internationally published author of several short stories in the horror and dark fantasy genres. His work has appeared in noted publications such as Morpheus Tales and Danse Macabre, as well as several anthologies. In addition, he reads submissions for several horror publications. He is presently working on his debut novel and plays Dungeons & Dragons at every opportunity. He can be found online at Facebook and Twitter @DWeaverWriter.

Gwendolyn Kiste is a speculative fiction writer based in Pennsylvania. Among other outlets, her work has appeared in LampLight, Nightmare Magazine, Flash Fiction Online, and Flame Tree Publishing's *Chilling Horror Short Stories*. She currently resides on an abandoned horse farm with her husband, two cats, and not nearly enough ghosts. *A Shadow of Autumn* is her first work as a professional editor. Find her online at gwendolynkiste.com.

Troy Blackford is a writer in his supremely early thirties living in the Twin Cities, Minnesota with his wife, a miniature human, two cats, and a new human on the way. He divides his time between writing, reading, conducting linguistic experiments on his offspring, and being stomped on by all members of his family save (usually) his wife. He has a number of works of fiction available wherever nearly all books are sold, and none available in places that show greater discernment. The most recent of these is his 2015 paranormal thriller, *Under the Wall*. He also has over twenty pieces of short fiction published by people other than himself. He hopes you have a ghoulishly enjoyable Halloween, this year and every other. You earned it.

Mike Watt is a journalist, author and filmmaker, best-known for his work for Fangoria, Femme Fatales, Cinefantastique and Sirens of Cinema Magazines. He is the author of the non-fiction *Fervid Filmmaking, Movie Outlaw*; the short-story collection *Phobophobia* and the novels *Suicide Machine* and *The Resurrection Game*. With Amy Lynn Best, he runs the company Happy Cloud pictures and wrote and/or directed and/or produced *The Resurrection Game, Splatter Movie: The Director's Cut, A Feast of Flesh, Demon Divas and the Lanes of Damnation* and *Razor Days*.

K.Z. Morano is a writer, a beach bum, and a chocolate addict. She's a certified bibliophile and her tastes range from Jane Austen to Edward Lee. She writes anything from romance and erotica to horror and SF, F, and WTF. K.Z.'s stories have appeared in various anthologies, magazines, and online venues since 2013. She is the author of *100 Nightmares*, a collection of 100 horror stories, each written in exactly 100 words, with over 50 illustrations. K.Z. currently resides in the Philippines. She blogs at theeclecticeccentricshopaholic.wordpress.com

Brooke Warra grew up and developed a deep fascination with the macabre in a fishing village in the Pacific Northwest with her very Finnish family. Her fiction has appeared in Under the Bed and Sanitarium Magazine among other outlets. She writes and lives with her two children near Phoenix, Arizona.

Tawny Kipphorn is a writer of supernatural and psychological suspense short stories and poems. She has been writing for nearly ten years, and is inspired by authors from the 1800s Romanticism period. She describes her poetic style as a combination of Edgar Allan Poe and Dr. Seuss. She has been published in Tales From The Shadow Realm, Inner

Sins, and Sanitarium Magazine. Aside from Literature, Tawny also has interests in cooking, spirituality, psychology, and the paranormal and the occult. She resides in the southern United States with her fiancé, fur baby, and lizard baby. Find her online at darkdoorpassages.wordpress.com.

COVER MODEL
Payden King has an avid love of science and enjoys finding beauty in the things that most people don't. Case in point: ever since first holding a Chilean Rose Hair tarantula two years ago, Payden has been collecting spiders. It should be no surprise that her favorite holiday is Halloween. She enjoys the mysterious ambiance surrounding the holiday, including the smell of autumn in the air, pumpkins and haunted houses, scarecrows and corn mazes, and of course the amazing color changes in the trees—and let's not forget pumpkin spice coffee! Payden is currently studying Forensic Anthropology at Mercyhurst University in Erie.

ILLUSTRATOR
Bill Homan is a New England native now living in the Pittsburgh area. A special effects artist, potter, photographer, and visual artist, he is also the long-suffering spouse of editor Gwendolyn Kiste. You can find him hiding in the shadows, fearfully wondering what project his lovely wife might rope him into next.

FURTHER HALLOWEEN READING

The End of Summer: Thirteen Tales of Halloween by J. Tonzelli

The October Country by Ray Bradbury

All Hallows' Evil, Editor Sarah E. Glenn, Mystery and Horror LLC

Made in the USA
Charleston, SC
29 September 2015